LEGEND OF LOVADA BRANCH

BOOK TWO: PANTHER GAP

LEGEND OF LOVADA BRANCH

BOOK TWO: PANTHER GAP

Karen Karper Fredette

Illustrated by Paul A. Fredette

ISBN- 13:9781090525727

Printed in the United States

All characters, events and places in this book are fictitious. Any resemblance between actual events, places and persons is coincidental.

Lovingly dedicated to Paul

Introduction

When a new book series appears in the world, questions arise that only time can answer. Will it become as "living" an experience for its readers as the writing of it has been for the author? Is it endowed with that rare quality of story and characters that it not only lingers in the minds of the readers (May they be many!) but raises lasting questions? A good novel, I believe, engenders more questions than it answers. Following the advice of Rainer Maria Rilke, let us live the questions now with the hope of someday living into the answers.

A work of fiction like this has been many years in formation and owes its life and final form to many events, to folks, near and far, whose lives have intersected mine, often unknowingly, as well as to the inherent evolution of the writer wrought by Life.

My special gratitude flows out to a unique people who have preserved their heritage and culture for centuries in the ancient mountains of western North Carolina. Their music, their language, their particular outlook on life provided me, as a writer, with the necessary context in which to set my particular inspiration.

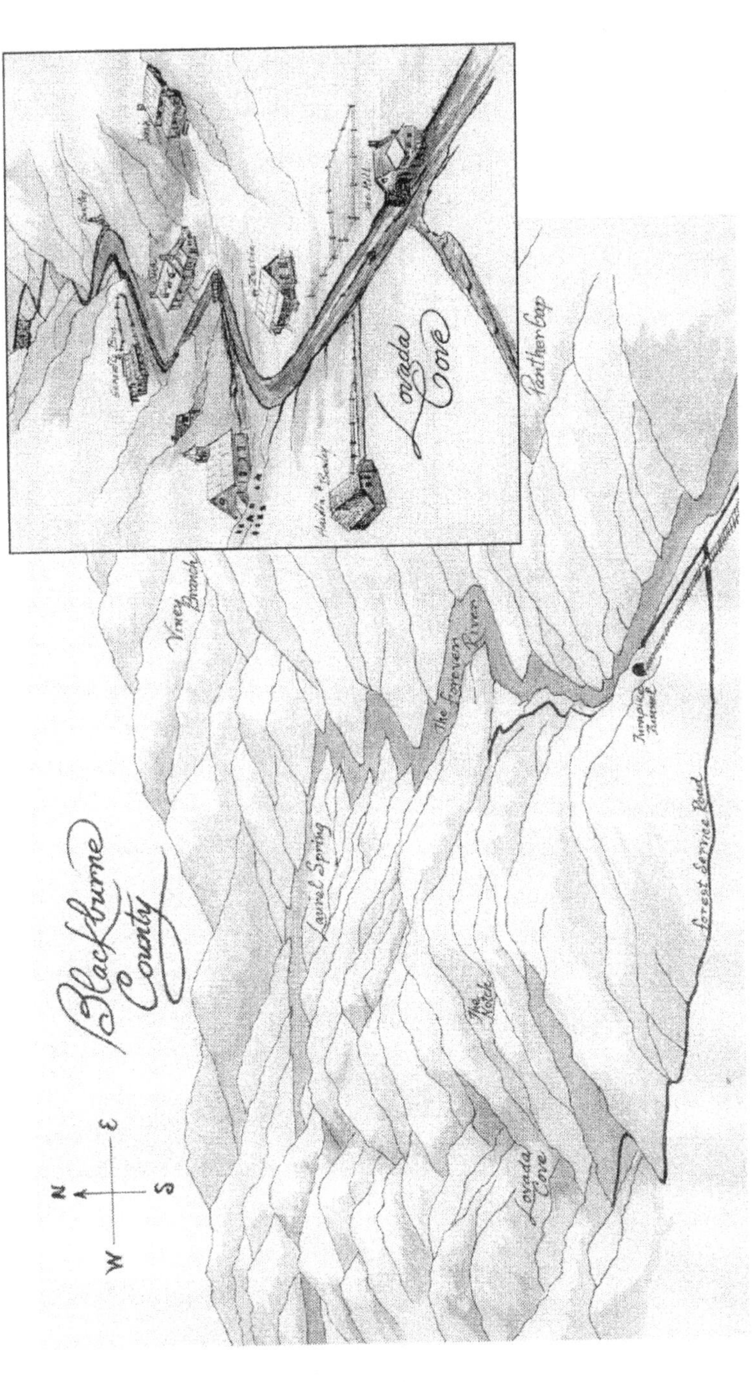
Blackburne County
N
E
S
W
Lorada Cove
Panther Gap
Viney Branch
The Forever River
Laurel Spring
The Notch
Lorada Cove
Turnpike Tunnel
Forest Service Road

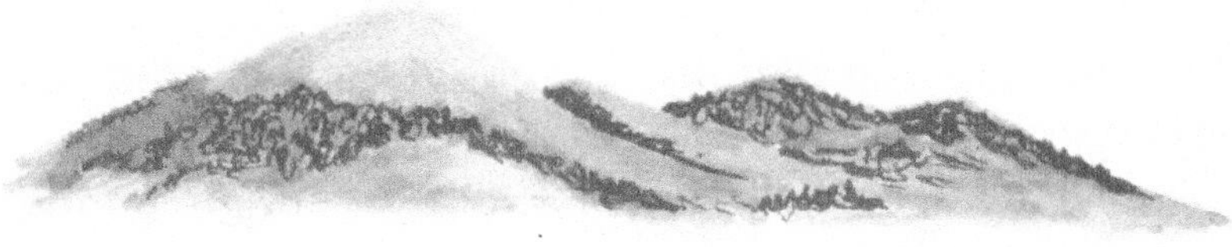

Prologue

"Kyle! Kyle Makepeace!" Wren panted, trying to capture the attention of her husband whose stocky figure was fast disappearing down the trail where dusk was creeping across the face of Unaka Mountain. They had been hiking most of the day with hardly a break and Wren was exhausted, her feet hurting and shoulders aching from her pack.

"Kyle!" she shouted again, exasperated that she couldn't break through his brooding concentration. "To hell with you!" she snapped as briars snagged her jeans, "I'm not going one step further, no matter who's dead." She yanked loose the straps securing her pack, letting it thump to the ground and slumped down beside it.

Wren had kicked off her boots and was massaging her aching feet when Kyle anxiously (and finally) woke to the fact that he was hiking alone.

Striding back, he demanded, "Wren? What's got into you?" as he peered down at the top of her drooping head. "We can't stop now! We've *got* to get back."

Angrily, Wren tossed her head up, a flinty gleam in her eyes. Her face was streaked with sweat and dirt, dark smudges under her eyes. "Kyle, I'm telling you I've gone my limit. Besides, we can't hike in the dark. What do you think I am, a damn mountain cat?"

A grin momentarily creased Kyle's drawn face as he pictured his feisty wife padding silkily through the forest, eyes gleaming green in the moonlight. "You'd make one hell of a pretty panther," he admitted and was rewarded with a remarkably catlike growl.

"We'll just go on until its dusk," Kyle urged. "I planned that we stop at the campsite we used on our way in."

"Oh, *you* planned, did you?" Wren repeated with a purr that told Kyle he'd once more put his boot in his mouth.

"Kyle," Wren added with exaggerated patience. "Look around you now. Can you see anything? Anything at all? It's *already* dark. What have you been thinking? Or haven't you?"

Startled, Kyle glanced into the trees along the trail. Shadows did indeed pool beneath them. Where had the day gone? Accustomed to extensive hiking, he'd kept up a steady rhythm along the comparatively easy trail down the mountain, his mind absorbed by the events of the past few days.

"Guess I've been lost back in The Cove," Kyle admitted sheepishly. He studied their surroundings more carefully and realized that Wren had thrown down her pack only yards from the clearing where he'd intended they would camp for the night.

"Okay, Wren, no further," Kyle agreed as he squatted beside her. He reached for her hand and before she could snatch it away, attempted to salvage what he could of their strained relationship. "I'm sorry I drove on so hard. These past days have... ", He groped for words and was relieved when Wren squeezed his fingers and nodded, biting her trembling lips. Grateful that Wren seemed mollified by his awkward apology, Kyle quickly dropped his pack and began collecting tinder and firewood before it turned totally dark.

Soon, tiny flickers of flame highlighted the broad planes of Kyle Makepeace's face as he blew on the incipient blaze and carefully fed it twigs and leaves. Although he knew Wren was right, he couldn't deny his uneasiness, fearing that any more time lost would just add to an already difficult situation. This would be the second night since the fatal mudslide. But it was only after Mencie, that ageless, seemingly omniscient, mountain woman, had forbidden them to return to Wren's Mamaw Zettie in The Cove, that Kyle and Wren had felt this strange urgency to return to Laurel Spring as quickly as possible.

Hastening down the mountain, everything within Kyle had hummed with awareness of the seismic shift taking place within him and his world. At this moment, as he watched the leaves and shavings curl and blacken in his fire, Kyle smiled grimly. All the plans he'd once had for his life were just as surely being turned to ash.

Beside him, Wren quickly opened their packs and groped around for cooking utensils and packets of dried food. Guided more by her ears than by sight, Wren found the small spring that trickled down the slope above them. Kyle noted how confidently she moved about the woods now. When they had last camped here – was it only five days ago? – Wren had huddled fearfully by the fire, twitching at every unfamiliar sound in the underbrush.

Tonight she appeared as comfortable on this untamed forest slope as Kyle himself. Half-Cherokee, he had spent several months of each year in the woods since he was old enough to carry a pack. Wren's newly acquired poise in the wilderness was one more sign of the monumental changes that she, too, had undergone in the past several days.

Only a few days ago, Wren had discovered her birth family and name and established ties with a grandmother she hadn't known existed. She also had been drawn deeply into the life of The Cove, a secluded community of elders unknown to the world at large. Among them she had undergone a stripping of all the defenses she had developed to cope with her anguish over being an abandoned child. Her quick anger, brisk professionalism, driving ambition to prove herself – all her defenses against this grief - had been demolished.

Until recently, only Kyle had been privy to Wren's profound vulnerability, her pervasive sense of inner hollowness. To her own lasting surprise and gratitude, Wren had discovered she could trust the compassion and gentleness that lay beneath the often impassive surface of this complex man, her husband for the past three years. This venture into the wilderness had been one expression of that trust.

After satisfying the edge of their hunger, Kyle and Wren now settled back to savor their "dessert" of dried fruit and nuts. Kyle threw some larger logs on the glowing embers and the low cooking fire blazed up, casting dancing shadows about the clearing. In the flickering light, the gravity on Kyle's face was sharply defined and his thick silvery hair, worn long and held in place with a headband, shimmered eerily. "Do I really know this man?" Wren asked herself, as she watched Kyle drop to the ground on the other side of the fire pit. She tried to peer into the shadows under his brow where his eyes flickered like live coals as he stared somberly into the flames.

During the past few days, Wren had been first shocked, then angry, to discover that Kyle had deliberately concealed much of his earlier life from her. For Kyle not only wore the mantle of a shaman of his father's people but was also an ordained priest in his mother's Christian faith. Furthermore he had consciously abandoned both sacred trusts for reasons Wren could not fully fathom. She had yet to deal with the mixed emotions aroused by this new knowledge. When she had met him, he was employed in a job training center in Laurel Spring, North Carolina.

Wren was startled from her reverie when Kyle, studying her from across the fire, asked softly, "Woman, what shall I call you now? What is your name for yourself? Are you Wren Linda Haggard, the foster daughter brought up by Glenda and Bill Haggard among their own brood? Or will you now claim your true family and heritage as Winnie Lovada Glenning? After what you've learned about me, do you still want to carry my name and be my wife, Wren Makepeace?"

Kyle's voice cracked and Wren stared back at him, still as a doe caught in a jacklight. Relentlessly, Kyle continued, his voice rising. "More than just your name is up for grabs, Wren. Everything is, everything! Do you realize how you are changing from day to day, becoming different from the woman I married? I don't know you. Who *are* you? *What* are you? And," Kyle's voice softened again, "most importantly, *how* are you, my dear?"

Touched to her core by this most caring of questions, Wren scooted around the fire to lean her head against Kyle's muscular shoulder. She sighed gently as his arm reached around and pulled her slender frame onto his lap. Briefly Kyle rested his chin on her reddish curls while Wren stroked his beardless cheek. "My Cherokee," she murmured fondly, grateful that Kyle had finally breached the silence in which they had hiked most of that May day and voiced questions she herself had been pondering about *him*.

Wren wanted to trust Kyle despite all she had learned about his past while they were together in the Valley of the Spring. That secret glen guarded the source of Lovada Branch, now known as Loverly Creek, the bold stream tumbling past their present campsite. But burdened now with untested knowledge of themselves and of each other, it felt like they should be introduced anew.

What would happen to their former life? F*ormer* life? Wren caught her breath sharply. Was that how she was now thinking of all the routines and responsibilities that had filled her world and defined who she was until now? Had she known what she now knew, when they set out on this "honeymoon hike" in search of some clues about her birth family, would she have gone? Had any one told her what awaited her and Kyle in the wilds of Unaka Mountain, she would simply not have believed them. They had walked into a living legend.

The "abandoned" community that had once flourished at the headwaters of Lovada Branch had proven to be far from deserted. Guided by the mysterious Mencie, who had assured them that no one *ever* found The Cove unless they were either sent there or summoned, Wren and Kyle had discovered an entire community of elders who were known only to a scattering of descendants "out in the world."

To their surprise, the couple had found themselves not only warmly welcomed but apparently expected by the vibrant seniors who inhabited The Cove. Their confusion deepened to dismay when they learned that The Cove stood in imminent danger through betrayal by one of its own and that Wren and Kyle were the chosen means of its preservation.

Thrust unwillingly through experiences which had seared and tested them, they had left the Cove carrying knowledge and responsibilities that would bring bereavement to one family, and challenge to others. For a necessary but brief period of healing and recovery they had been given this two day hike back to civilization and the life-changes looming ahead of them.

"Yes, we need to talk," Wren thought as she leaned against Kyle's chest and felt his steady heart-throb against her shoulder. She touched Kyle's lips lightly with her fingers and whispered in response to his outburst, "I really *don't* know how I am. For the first time in my life, I know *who* I am. I can now forgive my mother for leaving me as she did. She didn't intend it to be so. And I'm so sorry she died then and left most of us, especially Mamaw Zettie, to wait and grieve and never know the truth for so long. It's hard to understand how Locke could have kept it secret all those years... being my Mom's brother and knowing how his parents were anguishing. But like he finally said, he felt *that* anguish, terrible as it was, did not compare to the grief they would have experienced if they had known the real truth of what had happened to their Della ... through their other son."

"Porter." Kyle said grimly. He wasn't finding it at all easy to forgive a man who had raped his own sister and learning she was pregnant, had done nothing but try to save his own reputation. Della had died because she had tried to reach the Cove – and safety – too soon after their child's birth. She had left her baby, temporarily she thought, in the safe ward of the kind-hearted Haggard family which had sheltered her during the anxious months of her unwanted and shameful pregnancy. But Della's desperation had caused her to drive her body too hard and she had begun to hemorrhage on the trail. Mercifully, she had been found by Mencie before she died and was able to entrust the secret of her daughter's whereabouts to the fey guardian of The Cove.

Mencie, in turn, had informed Locke and given him the silver disk which signified Wren's hereditary role as Keeper of the Spring, source of Lovada Branch. Locke had delivered the disk to the Haggard family and faithfully concealed Wren's residence in the suburbs of Lashton from what he suspected was Porter's murderous intents. He had been successful for over thirty years.

Kyle, caught up in a mental replay of events of the past week, unconsciously crushed Wren's fingers in his grip as he recalled the horrendous night when he and Locke had raced through a storm-wracked woods to rescue Wren from a man she innocently thought of only as her uncle.

Wren stirred in Kyle's arms and squealed in pain. "Kyle! That's my hand you're crunching, not a rock."

"Sorry, honey. I was just remembering .... "

"Yes?"

"...that night you learned who Porter really was and he begged you to kill him."

"I nearly did, you know," Wren said quietly. "I hated him so much. He had raped my mother... in a way, he killed her. Then he went on to become such an upstanding man in the community, principal of the high school, father of three other children..., Wren faltered, "Kyle, even though I did wish him dead right then, I'm terribly sorry now."

"Sorry that you wanted to kill him?"

"That, yes, but even more that he *did* die and so horribly." Suddenly Wren turned her face into Kyle's chest and her strangled sobs quickly escalated into a howl of grief. Kyle held his wife's shuddering body tightly and stared hard into the fire, unaware of the tears streaking his own face. "Cry, honey, cry all you want," he whispered fiercely. "It is time."

For a while it seemed her tears would never cease but gradually Wren's sobbing checked. In strangled tones, she asked, "You know what hurts the most, Kyle? It's that I never knew them, never knew either one of them." Kyle nodded wordlessly as they both contemplated the empty spaces in Wren's life. She'd grown up an orphaned, unwanted child and her unsatisfied need to simply be someone's own, had left an ache nothing could ever completely erase.

Kyle could be empathetic but never fully appreciate Wren's grief. He and his twin brother, Crowe, had grown up in a tight family unit in Lowry, Massachusetts where his father had been a construction worker and his mother a nurse. Every summer, they had returned to his father's people on the Cherokee Boundary in North Carolina where he and Crowe had imbibed their Tsalago heritage and been trained in the woods lore that had distinguished their father. But it had all ended for Kyle the terrible year his brother had died from football injuries and his parents had perished in a house fire. Fiercely angry, nineteen year old Kyle had set out to avenge his loss on the God he held responsible.

Wren's anger he could understood very well. Her ability to forgive, when she had stood over the wreck of a man Porter had revealed himself to be, had shocked and shaken him. Such a capacity had something to do with that place, The Cove... with the assurance of Zettie that he and Wren would be watched over when she had sent them out into the night to save the community from betrayal and destruction. Kyle had felt powerful, praying presences surrounding them ... presences which still accompanied them on this homeward trail, Kyle suddenly realized.

He continued stroking Wren's rumpled hair, rocking her wordlessly as, emotionally drained, she rested against him. The logs on the fire shifted, sending out a shower of sparks that briefly reminded Kyle of eyes in the night. He felt Wren patting around his hips and reached back to pull out a handkerchief. She blew her nose and then jerked back abruptly.

"Whew! It's been a long time since this hanky has seen the inside of a laundry tub, Kyle Makepeace," Wren scolded.

Kyle scowled and then grinned sheepishly. "I keep it in my hunting jeans. Don't want the scent of fresh clothes to alert the critters."

"I'd say you would drive them off," Wren sniffed. "No wonder you come home so often with only half a roll of film shot."

"The woods aren't populated like they used to be ..." Kyle began defensively but stopped, suddenly alert to a change in the forest sounds around them. Wren felt his body stiffen.

"What is it?" she whispered, listening intently.

"Down there," Kyle indicated with a nod toward the gorge. "Something moving in the brush."

Wren heard heavy panting and caught a rank odor on the air. "B-b-bear?" she breathed.

"I think so," Kyle said softly. He closed his eyes, listening intently for another moment to the various sounds along the trail. Then, to Wren's surprise, Kyle relaxed, a wry smile touching his lips and called out, "Belva? That you?"

Sounds of scrabbling and cracking came up from the gorge where Loverly Creek flowed. Before Wren could leap up to join their food bag hanging from the tree branch overhead, Kyle squeezed her tightly and commanded, "Stay still. Stay low here with me. Don't run. Don't even move." Quivering Wren obeyed, her eyes fixed in the direction of the approaching noises.

Kyle called again, "Belva, come in if you please. I want you to meet someone."

Wren barely suppressed a scream when the brush parted and a black bear, four-foot high at the shoulder, padded into the light of their fire. The beast stopped, momentarily blinded by the light, and raised herself up to an impressive eight feet.

Enunciating each syllable soothingly, Kyle spoke directly to the behemoth towering over them, "Welcome, my friend."

He held out his hand, palm upwards in a gesture of peace. Then he touched Wren's chest, followed by his own. When he repeated the gestures, the bear cocked her head slightly.

"What *are* you doing? Wren whispered tensely.

"I'm trying to tell her you are my mate," Kyle responded as he continued to stare hard into the bear's small eyes.

This quaint formality tickled Wren despite her terror and she choked on a hysterical giggle. Belva snorted softly and lowered her head to focus her near-sighted eyes on the couple sitting against the tree.

"Great going, Wren," Kyle muttered from the corner of his mouth. Waving his hand in an apologetic gesture, he said gravely to the towering bear. "She didn't mean that the way it sounded."

When the black beast huffed, Kyle leaned toward Wren, "Please meet Belva, Wren. It is important for you to know her...and she, you. Belva is my totem." Wren bowed her head ever so slowly, feeling something akin to awe touch her as the great black bear stood before them with queenly dignity.

"Belva, why are you so far down the mountain? You're out of your territory, aren't you?" Kyle asked, "It isn't safe for you down here."

Seeming to shrug, the bear turned slowly and lumbered back down the bank toward the gurgling branch. Kyle frowned. "I don't like to see her so far out of her range. But she's going somewhere and far be it from me to stop her."

"Thank God!" Wren exclaimed as she began to breathe again. "Why did you call her Belva? Is she the one that nearly mauled you back in The Cove?"

"Yeh," Kyle admitted, "I was stupid and angry. She was angry too ... and had every reason to be. I had stumbled across the bodies of her twin cubs. If it hadn't been for Mencie..." Kyle's voice trailed off as he was caught up in another vivid memory.

Wren studied his face in the firelight. Kyle had told her the whole story of that incident already. She could enter his mind now with sympathy for the radical emotional surgery he had undergone through Mencie's ruthless probing of his deepest hurts and angers.

Wren stroked Kyle's clenched fist and felt his fingers relax and curl around hers in a beguiling way she recognized. She responded with a gentle squeeze and tilted her head for Kyle's searching mouth. No matter what had happened to both of them this past week, one thing in Wren's universe remained certain. She loved this man and believed in his love for her. Hungrily she returned his kiss. Kyle's husky suggestion that it was time to spread out their bedrolls further stirred her ardor.

"Do we need to set up the tent tonight?" she asked. Kyle studied the star-strewn sky visible through the tree branches and shook his head. As the fire died down to embers, they zipped their sleeping bags together and crawled in, undressing as they went. If there were any rocks or twigs beneath her,

Wren was unaware as Kyle spread his warm muscular body over hers. Clasping her arms around his neck, she drew him close. "I love you, Kyle Echota," she whispered and he responded tenderly, "And I, you, Winnie Lovada." Startled by his use of her newly recovered name, Wren stilled, uncertain and confused. How much did Kyle know of Winnie Lovada? How much did she?

Kyle, sensing Wren's withdrawal, stopped caressing her neck and shoulders to peer deeply into her eyes. Wren was staring at him in the dying light from their fire, questions flickering across her face. "Kyle," she whispered, "let me be Wren tonight. I don't know Winnie Lovada very well yet...and neither do you." Fiercely, she tangled her fingers in his hair and pulled his mouth down on hers. Tonight she was still Wren, but who she would become in days to come, would inevitably change even this most precious and intimate relationship.

Kyle yielded to her need even as unwanted emotions churned through his own heart. How would claiming his rejected past affect their marriage?

A questioning trill wakened them the next morning, a sweet prelude to the full dawn symphony that filled the misty air as the woods came to life, scented and fresh with full spring. Kyle rinsed the sleep from his eyes at the spring and noted how leafed out the larger trees were. Splashing more water on his face, he called out to Wren who was trying to balance a coffee pot over the coals she had stirred to life. "Today is the first day of June," he commented with surprise.

"A new month, a new life," Wren responded flippantly as she joined him at the spring. Her grin faded when she realized that their first task once they reached Blackburne County was driving over the mountain to Panther Gap where Porter's family lived to inform them of his death.

CHAPTER ONE

Wren and Kyle trotted down the rough slab steps marking the trail's end and were relieved to spot their red pick-up where Kyle had left it six days earlier. Wren, hurrying to toss her pack into the bed of the truck, suddenly paused. "It must have rained a good bit while we were gone, Kyle. Look how fresh these flowers are!" She pointed to the wake robins that they'd accidentally left on the hood. Kyle had plucked them when they'd parked, intending to tuck them into Wren's pack.

Kyle glanced over. "So much has happened this past week, it's surprising they haven't put out roots!" he commented, unlocking the cab and scrounging for the watch he had tucked into the glove box. Kyle shook the watch and held it to his ear, for it seemed to have stopped Monday, May 26th. But no, it was ticking steadily, reading 2:30 PM, the time of day he figured it should be. When Wren tossed the flowers past his nose and onto the dash, a shiver of premonition replaced his annoyance.

Hearing Wren grunt impatiently as she struggled to heave the rest of their gear into the truck, Kyle shrugged away his worry, strapped on the watch and hurried over to help her. Once on the blacktop road that wound down the mountain toward Laurel Spring, Kyle asked casually, "We agreed this morning that it's June 1st, didn't we?"

Turning toward Kyle with a puzzled frown on her face, Wren said, "Well, yeah. It's been a week, hasn't it, since we set out?" She twisted her fingers together tightly, "We need to get over to Porter's place as soon as we can. After all, it's been two days since we... since he ... was caught in the rock slide. Oh, God, Kyle, how are we going to tell his wife and kids what *really* happened? How can we even explain why it's taken us so long to get the word to them?"

Sharing Wren's concern, Kyle let the mystery of his (until now) accurate watch slip from his mind. "When Mencie sent us out, I think she said that Locke would meet us at the Glenning place, Porter's farm. I expect he'll be the one that will break the news since we don't really know Porter's family. It's funny, you know, how one can live six years in a small place like Blackburne County and not meet even a quarter of the folks."

Wren nodded slowly. "I wonder if we'll ever be anything more than outlanders to the people who've lived here all their lives."

"Likely we won't be, Wren, even if you are a Glenning," Kyle responded. "Folks around here just don't mingle with or trust others easily, even folk who have "come up" in the very next cove."

Wren nodded in agreement. "Families living up in Viney Branch seem wary of folks from over in Panther Gap and people from Laurel Spring don't have much to do with folks from Sandy Mush! No wonder there's little welcome for the Hispanic families that are starting to settle around here!"

"Haven't you noticed that none of the Hispanics are actually living in Blackburne County, Wren? Even those who work here have settled their people just over the county line in that old drover's encampment along the Forever River," Kyle observed softly.

Distressed, Wren ran her hands through her hair and frowned as she felt how lank it was. They'd hiked fast and hard to make it off the trail in time to go out to Porter's farm that same day. But now she felt so grubby she hoped they could stop by their home in Laurel Spring for a quick shower before facing the ordeal ahead.

Just as she opened her mouth, Kyle swung the Ford into Billy's Gas Station and jumped out to fill up. He pulled his money clip out of his pocket and strode into the cluttered office next to the open bay where Billy was stretched out beneath a dented pick-up.

"Jest throw hit down near the cash register," Billy drawled. "I can't let loose of this here thingamajig."

Kyle nodded and tossed a ten on the counter. A breeze flipped the pages of the calendar dangling on a nail. "Better change your calendar over to June, Billy. Wouldn't want you to be a month behind with your billing!" Kyle joked, for the mechanic was notoriously casual about book-keeping. "It's a good thing most folks around here feel sorry for your family and keep track of their own credit so you can stay in business."

Billy rolled out from under the truck, wiping his hands on an oily rag. "Don't try to tell me hit's June a'ready, man. We was goin' out to the Glenning's fer the Memorial Day doin's this evenin'." He lifted his chin to the sign on the door. Kyle read the magic marker notice that was obviously printed by one of Billy's kids and his breath hitched. "Closed after 4PM today, Memorial Day."

"Thought that was Monday," Kyle muttered, feeling his neck hairs raise again. "It IS Thursday, isn't it?" Billy kept rubbing his hands, the grin on his face fading a bit as he shook his head. "Better not be," he groaned, "my kids would be mighty put out if they'd a'missed the doin's, not to mention my Rilla's feelin's! She's been bakin' up a storm all weekend."

After filling up, Kyle jumped into the cab and slammed the truck door, startling Wren out of a light doze. She rubbed her tired eyes. "What are you all upset about?" she murmured vaguely.

"Don't ask!" Kyle snapped.

"Okay, okay," Wren snapped back. "What I really want to know is if we can take time to stop at the house and duck under a shower before going out to see Porter's family."

"We can take all the time you want," Kyle bit off and muttered under his breath, "we seem to have more time than we should." He stared straight ahead to discourage any further comment from Wren. Something was strange, something he didn't want to explore any further at this point. A couple minutes later, he obligingly nosed the truck over the bridge that formed part of their driveway. It *would* feel good to get cleaned up before facing the Glenning's.

Kyle was carrying their back packs into the kitchen when Miz Brazilla, their neighbor across the road, hollered out to Wren. "How come you'ns back so soon? Figured you was goin' to be hikin' a week. Ain't thet what you said?"

"Well, we did, 'Zilla," Wren called back. Before she could engage in further conversation with their nosy neighbor, Kyle hustled Wren into the house, firmly shut the door and leaned against it, breathing hard. Looking deep into Wren's eyes, Kyle spoke carefully, "Something is "almighty strange", as they say in these parts. Here in town, all the folks think it is Memorial Day."

"But that was on the 29th," Wren protested. "It's the first of June…isn't it?"

Kyle pulled hard on his nose. "So we figured, hon. But how can watches and calendars and people all tell the same lie? It can't be just a bad joke on us."

Wren backed out of Kyle's grip. "You mean that it really is just Monday …*here*?" she stuttered. "B-b-but that can't be. We started out last Friday, spent the first night on the trail and met up with Mencie around noon on Saturday. Then we slept at the Bentley place after I met Mamaw Zettie."

Kyle took over, counting on his fingers. "So it was Sunday when we went to the Meeting at the church. Later that night,

Mencie called us out and we ended up at the old Waitsel homestead and...and Della's grave. The next day, Monday, I met up with Belva..."

Wren interrupted, "and that evening, we all gathered at Oma's. Zettie sent us out into the storm that night... and the rockslide came down on us. So it was Tuesday when we told Zettie about Porter and slept at her house that night. We went to the Spring on Wednesday...

"...and started hiking back out at Mencie's 'suggestion'," Kyle added wryly. "We slept on the trail that night, last night, I mean. So today IS Thursday....isn't it?"

"But you say folks here in town are talking like it's only Monday, Memorial Day...like we were only gone three days!" Wren whispered, as she gripped Kyle's shirt.

"It's...it's like the days in The Cove didn't count," Kyle said slowly, reluctantly. "Naw, can't be...let me work this out." He rubbed his forehead thoughtfully and then, before Wren could stop him, he grabbed her jeans, unsnapped them and pulled them down roughly.

Wren stumbled backward and fell into an easy chair. "Kyle! What on earth...?"

Kyle was kneeling, stroking the dark bruise, now turning yellow-green at the edges, on Wren's shin. "It's healing, looks like it's about three, maybe four days old. The rock from the cairn fell on you Sunday night, didn't it, Wren?"

Wren said nothing, only ran her fingers lightly over the ugly bruise. Mencie had put a plantain poultice on it right away which had eased the worst of the pain. It was still quite tender though. Kyle sat back, rocking on his heels. He didn't like what the facts were telling him, didn't like it one bit. He needed time, time to think about what it might mean. In addition, he had some serious questions to ask Ol' Gaither when he caught up with that wily gentleman.

Slapping his hands on his knees, Kyle gave Wren a grim look which she knew meant "Subject closed!"

"Let's get our showers and be gone," he muttered.

An hour later, gravel sprayed as Kyle braked his Ford 150 behind Porter Glenning's barn. Stepping down from the cab, he searched for Wren's Honda Civic among the vehicles haphazardly pulled up into the yard. Her small taupe car always stood out among the usual collection of vans and pickups favored by folks in Blackburne County. When he didn't see it, Kyle pulled absently on his nose, frowning as he pondered his options.

Wren had left the house before he did, saying she needed to pick up a pie to take to the Glenning's. Kyle's lips quirked in a slight grin. "Shy Wren," he thought. "It's always easier to arrive at a strange place with a gift of food in hand. If she'd had time, she would have baked it herself. In things like this, she's so 'country'."

Kyle folded his arms over his chest and leaned against his truck. At the back of his mind this perplexing "time warp," as he was beginning to call it, was still distracting him. He had hurried over the ridge to the Glenning place because he wanted to get the delivery of the news of Porter's death behind them. Should he go ahead without Wren? No, he didn't think so. She was much more intimately involved in all this than he. Locke should be here, too, somewhere in the noisy crowd.

Kyle spotted a knot of men and older boys in clean jeans and overalls, huddling behind a tottering woodshed. He knew all of them by name at least and decided to find out what they were about. As he sauntered over, wiping his sweaty hands on the seat of his pants, most of the men acknowledged Kyle with a nod or lifted hand. Despite being an "outlander," Kyle had earned their acceptance and respect during the six years he had worked at the Center in Laurel Spring. Just as he entered their circle, another man, carrying a black leather bag, hurried around the opposite corner of the shed.

"Well Doc, we ain't got much time," Creed Gunter greeted him somberly. "The wimmen got the other'n up at the house. They'll be lookin' for this 'un afore long."

"Did you get what we need?" Doc Tanner asked, as he snapped open his case and pulled out some instruments.

"Liston went for it jest a while back," Denver, a boy of fifteen, offered diffidently.

"Aw, he's bin gone more'n an hour," his older brother Hershall countered roughly, giving him a shove. Kyle observed the boys with a troubled heart. He wasn't certain that Denver Ray Glenning should be part of these doings, whatever they were, but he knew Porter wasn't there to say otherwise. He suspected that this kid had just pushed himself into the mix of older men who were staying carefully out of sight of the big house....and their wives.

Doc turned to Creed, a small swarthy man with a bushy black moustache. "Where are you keepin'er?"

"We got 'er iced down and covered with a quilt. Woots here got this'un away from Cenia. We got to git it back afore they miss it." The other men in the circle nodded anxiously.

"Hey, Liston's drivin' in now," Hershall announced with nervous importance. A bearded man jumped out of a pickup and hurried round the corner of the shed.

"Well?" Doc asked sharply.

"I just got plumb lucky. It took some huntin' 'round to find fellers who would even admit to have'n any. This stuff is *really* stout, best I've ever... tasted. Whoo-ee! They'd only sell me but this one little jug."

Doc brushed off his hands and held a large syringe up to the light. Poking a long needle through the cork on the demijohn Liston proffered, he filled the syringe. "Okay, boys, let me at'er." Kyle trailed along, a thrill of apprehension running up his back.

Denver, scurrying ahead of the men, tugged open the woodshed door. Kyle's nostrils twitched at the pungent odor of wet sawdust and ancient hog.

"Out of the way, boy," Creed ordered as he thrust Denver back and strode over to the large blanket-covered bundle in the corner. "Iverson? You got the light?"

"Sure do," a thin man responded as he hitched up his jeans and flicked on a hand-held trouble light.

Carefully, Creed peeled back the heavy quilt to reveal the pale green skin of a watermelon, glistening with moisture from the ice packed around it.

Doc Tanner studied it briefly. "It's bigger than I expected. I'll need more of that corn liquor, Liston." He poked the syringe deeply into the melon and depressed the plunger slowly. Then he refilled it and pierced the other end of the green football. "That should do," he muttered, "it jest needs a little time to work through all the meat."

Worth, silent until now, rubbed his grizzled crew cut. "Iverson," he drawled, "you shure hit's ripe enough? Hit's mighty early in the year for watermelon."

"Worth, I know what I'm about. Don't my boy, Milt, work produce at Shingle's? He tole me bout this first shipment of melons comin' up from south of the border."

"Mexican watermelon!" Creed growled and spat on the ground. "Don't know but what we've just wasted a jug of good liquor, Doc. Do you think it'll take? I ain't never trusted a' one of them brownies' that don't know no English." Kyle noted uneasily that the naked scorn in Creed's tone was approved by vigorous nods from a number of the men.

"So why you workin' them in your 'bacca fields, Creed?" Iverson challenged. "Wouldn't be s'prised if none of them trusted *you* neither!"

Worth cut in, "You know why, Ive? It's 'cause he cain't get his girls out on the setter no more." He added with a snigger, "Ever since their Mama started workin' at the sweater factory, she saw there was somethin' more to life than grubbin' and choppin' 'bacca. Creed's Norie is sister to my Cenia and I heard them talkin'. They's been civil war at Creed's place for near on a year now."

"Sounds more like a revolution to me," Iverson teased and punched Creed's arm.

"Keep my family life out of this," Creed snarled. "I kin run my wimmen anyway I want. Becky and Lisa are just too busy – they're goin' to cheer leadin' camp agin this summer."

"They're good, too!" Denver broke in fervently. "Why when they do those cartwheels and their bitty skirts flip .... Yeow, Hershall, what you hittin' on me fer?" Denver swung round to shove his older brother but Hershall ducked swiftly through the door, whooping. "Jest you wait 'till Pa gits here. He'll tell you what fer."

Creed glowered after the boys, his face a stunned cross between fatherly pride and paternal anxiety. Kyle, too, watched the boys, knowing sadly that they could be enjoying their last few minutes of carefree boyhood. They'd be growing up mighty fast before the afternoon was over.

Iverson broke Kyle's train of thought. "So where *is* Porter? It's his place and his party. Not like him to leave a thing like this to Vestie."

"I asked Vestie when I came in," Doc Tanner offered, "but she wouldn't say much. I could see she was worried though. Admitted he's not usually gone this long."

"Ain't that a mite strange?" Iverson asked cynically. The other men smirked. It was common knowledge among them that the local principal often went into Lashton to spend a night or two at a whorehouse. So long as he kept his hands off their women they had no quarrel with where or how he spent his time.

"Last I saw Porter, he was talkin' to some of them forest service fellers in Laurel Spring – that weren't so long ago,"

Worth offered. "He seemed almighty worked up about somethin'."

"Think he'd be back fer the doin's," Doc commented, pursuing Iverson's puzzled observation. "Far as I can see, Porter never leaves anything to Vestie except the farm work and... Delphie." He hesitated, eying Kyle speculatively as if weighing how much he could trust this outsider.

Kyle waited impassively, wondering if he had passed enough tests to be allowed into some of the more personal areas of the lives of these private mountain folks.

The other men watched Carson Tanner, who as one of their own, could indicate how far "in" Kyle might be allowed. Doc shook out his syringe, drawling slowly, "Well now, Vestie's a shy sort of woman, not one to put herself forward. She almost never leaves the farm place here back of Panther Gap. Whether it's her choice or Porter's, I never quite worked out.

"Whenever I come out to doctor one of their cows, Vestie don't say much beyond what pertains to the trouble. If it's cold, she might offer me a cup of coffee but I don't often take her up on it. A country vet knows better than to set with another man's woman 'lessen that man's in earshot. Especially when she's a pretty one, like Vestie. Most times Porter is still at the high school with the boys."

"For shore, Porter ain't the sort you'd want to git riled up," Woots added significantly.

Kyle suddenly decided to step out of the woodshed, lest his face involuntarily reveal just how recently he had witnessed the truth of those words. He squinted up towards the large house set at an angle overlooking a grassy slope. The long front porch and numerous dormers gave it a hospitable air.

Doc was just a step behind him. "Hard to believe Porter built that almost single-handed except for Vestie," he mused. "Porter worked like a demon at it, driven-like. Fact is, he does everything that way."

Porter had become principal of the county high school, not so much because he was an outstanding teacher, but because of his deserved reputation for fierce discipline in his classes and with the football team he had coached to several local championships.

Kyle had picked up that folks generally admired Porter Glenning and considered his sons as rowdy but good kids. The boys, as driven as their Pa, were certainly one reason that their school football team had won the state championship this past year. But Kyle had never heard anything about a daughter.

He studied Tanner from the corner of his eye before asking curiously, "What's said about this Delphie?"

Doc Tanner glanced back at the men who were still milling about the melon, taking bets on how drunk a person could get on its ripe, red meat. "No one knows much about the girl," he began carefully. "Folks mostly figure she's "slow" since Porter's never sent her to school. Looks to be about six now but I know she's close on to nine years old. I've only seen her a few times myself, just long enough to know she's a mute." He flicked his fingers at a squirrel scampering across the porch roof. "That there's one of her pets. Seems to have a way with animals."

When Kyle cocked a questioning eye, Carson Tanner added, "Whenever Vestie has a hard time bringing in a cow from the pasture for a check-up, she sends Delphie out into the field. Without making a sound, that young'un can somehow "call up" the fractious critter and lead her over to the gate. Then she turns and runs like the wind towards the woods. Don't expect to see her today. Delphie never turns up when other folks are around. Not unless Vestie plays."

"Plays?" Kyle questioned.

Iverson, who had quietly joined the two men, burst in with disbelief, "You ain't never heard Vestie play? Folks here are always mighty pleased when Vestie picks up her dulcimer or fiddle. She's got her a right strong singin' voice, clear as a bird, and she knows *all* the ol' love songs, as we call' em. Her Granny Bureda done taught her."

"She has a gift, no doubt of that," Doc corroborated. "Everyone 'cept Porter seems to notice." He shook his head. "One of the best parts of this gathering is when Vestie joins the rest of the pickers and singers on the front porch. She'll sit there with that dulcimer in her lap, real quiet for awhile, not moving a muscle until suddenly her hands begin dancing over the strings. The rest of us just stop playing and wait. Pretty soon, she'll tilt up her head, listening it seems until the music calls it out of her, and then she starts to singing."

Iverson nodded appreciatively, "Her voice jest sails up and over you, liltin' and bright, with those trills and breaks only real ballard singers can do. It's like hearing her Granny Bureda all over again. Doc here figures Vestie's one of the best of the old-timey singers he's ever heard. And he's heard a'plenty."

Doc cleared his throat. "It's true. I pick the banjo myself and am usually part of every frolic around. There's none better than Vestie when it comes to mountain singing. Most times, I play with Porter's brother, Locke. Now there's a man what has a sweet way with a fiddle. I expect we'll see him today though it's rare for him to come out here. Porter and Locke, they had a falling out over something years ago and Locke usually keeps to his side of the county, looking after the family farm near Viney Branch where they'd all come up."

When Iverson moved on toward the house, Doc lowered his voice, "I figure that Locke comes to hear Vestie sing. There's something in the way he looks at her... sad, maybe, or angry. Once in a while when Vestie's singing one of those long love songs, Locke will pick up his fiddle and join her, playing a counterpoint around her voice that's as sweet as a lover's kiss. He doesn't do it if Porter's in earshot, though."

"I was away at veterinary school when Porter was courting Vestie so I don't know much of that history, but I expect my Maudie does." Doc added with a slight grimace, "That woman of mine knows all the gossip of the Gap. No, make that all of the county, for the past forty years. Makes me wonder if she don't have a built-in scanner. You don't want to get her started..."

Doc watched his matronly wife now as she bounced down the porch steps with Norie, Creed's wife. The two women were carrying a long cloth to spread over a table set up beside the house. Even from this distance, the men could see her mouth moving animatedly.

Just then a dusty green pickup pulled in where other vehicles were clustered and Locke stepped out, looking haggard and disheveled. Doc frowned, "Locke looks like he's just been turned loose by a love sick bear. Don't appear to have his fiddle with him neither."

Kyle shifted back toward the house, not wanting to engage in any conversation about Locke. It seemed to him that Doc Tanner was in the same league as his wife so far as local gossip went. They both watched with interest as Locke headed toward the woods instead of going into the house, or joining the other men lounging around the beer cooler.

"Strange." Doc mused, leaning heavily on a nearby fence rail. "Would he be looking for Delphie? Whatever for?"

Kyle strolled away without answering when he saw Wren's Civic pull in behind Locke's truck. As Kyle approached his wife, Creed muttered, "I din't expect to see them Makepeace's at this doin's. Only those what's come up here, should come out here."

Iverson needled him, "Hey, Creed. They only live ten miles over the mountain in Laurel Spring. Ain't that local enough fer ya?"

"Ive, you know what I mean. Them folks only just got here five, six years back. They ain't one of us."

Norie and Maudie stopped smoothing out the table cloth to stare silently as Kyle and Wren headed up the walk to the front porch. The level of chatter in the house diminished noticeably when they reached the steps. Kyle took Wren's cold hand into his own as he pulled open the screen door, without bothering to knock. This was going to be tough. He hadn't counted on half the county being here when they broke the news to Vestie and the boys ... and Delphie, he added hastily to himself.

He felt Wren tensing as a number of unsmiling faces turned toward them as they stepped into the front room and he fought a strong urge to cut and run. This wasn't the time ... not with all these folks here. But as Kyle squeezed Wren's hand, he was encouraged to see her lips set stubbornly as she scanned the room for Vestie. Kyle barely knew what the woman looked like, having only glimpsed her a few times in the cab of Porter's truck.

"I'm...we're looking for Vestie," Wren began, her voice cracking slightly. A tall, slender woman in jeans and a man's white shirt strolled in from the kitchen. A thick braid of dark red hair fell down her back. Kyle was struck by her graceful hands that she was wiping on a towel. He was also startled by something else he couldn't quite put his finger on. But as Vestie came into the light, Kyle felt like he was looking over Mamaw Zettie's shoulder at the old photos she treasured. Vestie bore an uncanny resemblance to Della Lovada, Wren's mother. They could have been sisters.

Such resemblances among the mountain folks were not hard to explain given the isolation of the region and the limited social life they had until the middle of the twentieth century. Everybody was kin to everyone else and Kyle had cautioned Wren, when she'd moved to Laurel Spring, to never "bad mouth" anyone because a third-cousin, a grand-niece or an in-law from three marriages ago was likely to be one of the folks who would hear her remarks – remarks that would be swiftly passed on and never forgotten.

Porter – and it sickened Kyle to realize it – had picked a wife who looked like his dead sister. Wren was struggling to find her voice, when Vestie came forward, apprehension darkening her eyes. "You come with news of Porter, ain't you," she said with certain prescience. When Wren nodded, the other women began to close protectively around Vestie.

Without taking her eyes off Wren, Vestie lifted her hand and asked, "Will someone please find Hershall and Denver Ray? Tell'em to come to the house... *now*!"

"Locke's also here, Vestie," Kyle put in. "He drove in after me and headed straight out to the woods. I'm not sure why."

A ghost of a smile touched Vestie's pale lips. "He's agoin' for Delphie, I would say. He knows where to find her." Even as she spoke, Locke strode in through the kitchen holding a little girl by the hand. Tangled strawberry blond hair framed a small smudged face with large, questioning eyes. "Doe eyes," Kyle thought, as he registered her soft brown stare and slightly flared nostrils.

Vestie reached out and pulled Delphie close to her hip. Hershall and Denver Ray clattered noisily up the porch steps, the screen door banging behind them.

"Hey, Ma, what you want us fer?" Hershall demanded angrily, before he noticed the puzzling tableaux in their front room. Locke stepped forward, suggesting, "Vestie, whyn't you and the boys come into the sun parlor with us?"

Vestie merely nodded and herded her brood ahead of her into a room of windows and light. A hand carved dulcimer lay on a round white table and even in his agitated state, Kyle couldn't help but admire its workmanship. Locke, following after Wren and Kyle, stood in the doorway, effectively blocking a horde of curious women from walking in with them.

"Sit down, Vestie," he said gently as Kyle pushed a wicker rocker toward her. Without taking her eyes off her brother-in-law, Vestie obeyed, gracefully settling her long-limbed body into the chair and pulling Delphie between her knees. The two boys moved around behind the chair, eyes anxiously scanning the faces of their uncle and the two strangers with him.

Something about their mother's gravity communicated itself to them and their usual arrogance disappeared, leaving unease on suddenly young faces.

Locke rubbed his hands down the front of his mud-stained coveralls. "Vestie, you know where Porter's been these last few days?"

"Said somethin' was going on in The Cove," she whispered. "Somethin' happen there, Locke?"

Locke looked down at the braided rug on the floor and rumbled gruffly, "Yeh, Vestie, it shore did. I 'spect you knew Porter was involved with forest service takeover of the federal lands back there?"

Vestie's shock spoke volumes but Hershall and Denver smirked.

"Wail, it seems Porter has been leadin' some men in to mark the timber and lay out a loggin' road. What he din't know was they'd already laid the dynamite to blast out the rock bars that cut across the access." The little family, clustered around the rocker, sucked in a sharp breath.

"Shit!" Hershall shouted, "You tryin' to tell us he got hurt, hurt bad mebbe?"

"Hesh, Hershall Lincoln," Vestie hissed as her eyes, a fiery cobalt blue, raked over Locke, Kyle and Wren.

Locke continued grimly, "The three of us were there, Vestie," and he nodded toward Kyle and Wren. "There was a major thunderstorm going on and we think it somehow tripped the timer for the blasts. They were sequenced and Porter thought he knew what would happen next. He pushed us into a gully but before....before he could jump in after us, all hell broke loose.

"Seemed like half the mountain started to slide – tons of loose rock up there – trees falling every which a'way. Dirt and boulders and branches were flying straight at us. Cause we were down in the gully, most of it flew over our heads but

Porter, he ….," Locke paused and licked his dry lips. "He got caught, buried in that avalanche.

"Vestie, trust me." Locke's eyes pleaded for understanding, "There was nothing we could do. It all came so fast. It was dark … and raining. We crawled up through the mess as soon as things had stopped movin' but we din't see Porter nowhere. Folks come out from the Cove as soon as it was light but we couldn't find anything of him."

Denver banged his fist on the back of the rocker. "No! He's okay, he's okay. Nothin' kin hurt my Pa. He's… he's jest hurt and wanderin' in the woods. I'm goin' to look for him and I'll find him, I'll …."

Locke looked compassionately at his nephew but would have moved quickly to block his escape from the room if Vestie hadn't grabbed her son's hand firmly. "No, Denver Ray, don't you go out there and risk me losing you, too. The folks at the Cove know every inch of those woods and if they searched and didn't …"

Vestie turned back to Locke, "Was Mencie there? Did *she* look? What'd *she* say, Locke?"

The anguish on Locke's sunburnt face deepened. "She was there, Vestie, I think even before we were able to get out of the gully. She didn't look for Porter. She didn't have to 'cause she already knew where he was… under that rockslide." He paused and let out a long breath, his eyes traveling slowly over his brother's stunned family.

Seeming to draw on his last reserve of energy, Locke offered, "When you're ready, I'll take you there – Hershall and Denver and Delphie – and Mencie will show youn's the place. You can mark the spot and mebbe it'll comfort you some."

Delphie's eyes had been traveling back and forth between Locke and her mother as they talked. Now she turned her face into Vestie's shoulder and slid her arms around her mother's neck. Vestie hoisted the child onto her lap and stroked her tangled hair. Some wordless communication passed between them before Vestie looked up at Locke, a question flitting across her face. "When did all this happen, Locke?"

"Bit ago." he admitted uneasily.

"Whatcha sayin', Uncle Locke," Hershall burst out. "Pa's bin gone and you din't tell us afore this?"

Locke shook his head. "Couldn't git here, son. We spent all the day huntin' fer him...and then, then I had to go tell Ma. I know it don't make a whole lot of sense...none of it does," Locke muttered softly. He nodded toward Kyle and Wren, who stood arm in arm, regarding the little family with deep compassion. "Thought it might help to have them with us since they saw it all, too."

Kyle was inwardly congratulating Locke on a difficult job well done. He'd managed to tell the story truthfully and, hopefully, in a way that wouldn't raise too many questions about what he hadn't said. It was going to be hard enough to explain why the four of them were out on the mountain at night in a storm. He knew Locke was determined to keep the whole of the sordid truth from coming out.

Stormy anger in Hershall and Denver's eyes didn't bode well, though. Even as he registered their growing fury, Kyle wondered at Vestie's apparent calm. Was she just in shock, not fully absorbing the facts? Or had she had some premonition of what was coming?

As if in response to Kyle's unspoken thoughts, Vestie stirred and said softly, "I – we- knew somethin' happened the night of the storm."

"You did?" Wren broke in.

Vestie regarded the younger woman with eyes older than her years. "You jest know, you jest *know* when your world's agonna' change, honey. Delphie and me, we knew, didn't we?" She touched her child's shoulder gently and the little girl looked up at Wren. Again Kyle, was struck with the child's doe-like eyes – wild and knowing and shy, all at once. His heart turned over for her diminutive figure reminded him of what

Wren would have looked like at her age. This little girl was her half-sister, after all. Did Wren see it, he wondered?

Latching on to some focus for his hurt and anger, Hershall glared at Kyle and Wren and spat out, "What youn's got to do with us?"

Locke stirred, taking his eyes from Vestie, to address Hershall. "Like your Ma said, there was somethin' goin' on in The Cove and it touched your family direct. Did your Pa ever tell you boys about our sister, your Aunt Della, who died afore you boys was born?"

Hershall and Denver shook their heads.

"Nah, he ain't never said nothin' bout youn's havin' a sister," Denver admitted cautiously. The boys seemed to be circling this idea like a baited trap that could snap closed at any moment, sensing that they might hear something unwanted about a father who, to them, was everything a man should be.

"Vestie?" Locke asked.

Vestie nodded slowly, lowering her eyes to Delphie's grubby hands in her lap. Her shoulders slumped a little. "I heard thet name," she whispered, "plenty of times. Didn't know who this Della was though. Thought she might've been some gal Porter courted afore he went off to college, someone he still had feelin's fer. Sometimes in his sleep, he'd mumble "Della" and add somethin' like 'sorry, so sorry'. Or he'd call out her name when we..." Vestie caught herself as she suddenly remembered her sons leaning over her shoulders.

Kyle felt Wren sag slightly against him and could guess her pity for this woman who, as far as Kyle could tell, was a mere stand-in for another woman who haunted her husband and cut him off from ever seeing her for who she really was.

Locke, so steady until now, suddenly choked and turned away. The deep red flush climbing his neck bespoke a powerful rage which Kyle thoroughly understood. It was time they took over the rest of this sorry narrative. But before he could formulate his words, Wren took a step forward.

"Vestie?" she began softly. "I don't know how much Porter told you about his sister. I don't know all that much myself, mostly just what Mamaw Zettie told me a few days back. Vestie, Della was my mother. But I never knew her or anything about her. She never told my foster parents her last name ... jest that she'd named me Winnie Lovada after her Mamaw and that Lovada was a traditional middle name in her family."

All the time Wren was speaking, Vestie's fierce cobalt eyes never left Wren's face. Kyle didn't doubt that Vestie was putting the facts together with what she already knew about her conflicted husband. Wren was more than just his niece. Vestie sighed deeply, tears suddenly obscuring the blue of her eyes. Rubbing the back of her hand over her cheek, she said softly, heavily, "So Della had her a daughter."

"I guess that makes me your niece," Wren added hesitantly.

"And much more," Kyle thought grimly to himself. While the adults in the room grappled silently with unspoken facts, the boys were studying Kyle and Wren with narrowed eyes. They suspected there was more to the story than the words they were hearing. But they were primarily absorbed in trying to grasp the enormity of their father's death, a death that made no sense to them.

"How come you know so much about our Pa?" Hershall asked suspiciously. "How do we know you're tellin' us the truth? How do we know it happened the way you said it did? How come you're livin' and he ain't? How ..."

Locke cut in sharply, "Hershall, son, let it be. We tole you what happened. Your Pa was tryin' to save us. He did but got caught hisself. You know how fast things go once a rock slide gits started. There was nothin' could be done," he finished helplessly.

Kyle could all but feel Locke's ache to touch Vestie who was sitting stunned, surrounded by her children. Quietly Delphie slipped off her mother's lap and went over to the table where the dulcimer lay. She looked back once at Vestie, then picked it up and carried it over to lay it on her lap. It appeared to Kyle this was not the first time the child had sought to comfort her mother with music.

Vestie looked down at the instrument on her knees as if she didn't recognize it. But Kyle could see her fingers quiver automatically. She plucked first one string, and then another. A poignant whisper of minor chords gradually evolved as Vestie's hands stroked the much loved instrument. Delphie curled up on the floor, leaning against her mother's long legs. She began to pat her knees comfortingly and Vestie, touching the child's head briefly, whispered, "Thank ye, Delphie."

The boys, however, refused the subtle invitation to mourn and pushing past their uncle, stalked out stony faced and silent.

As if this were a signal, the group of women who had been listening breathlessly behind Locke's broad back, suddenly broke out in shocked exclamations. Kyle could hear some of them hurrying off, eager to be the first messengers of bad news that would affect the whole county, not just the Glenning family and their neighbors in Panther Gap. The consolidated high school in Laurel Spring where Porter had been principal drew youngsters from all over Blackburne County.

When Locke turned to follow his nephews, some of the women, Maudie first among them, pushed past him to hug on Vestie, voicing grief and shock. Vestie, at first, continued to drift in the world her music set up around her.

Suddenly she stopped fingering the strings and gasped, "Zettie! Does Mamaw Zettie know? Oh, the poor woman. She was so proud of Porter. We ought to go to her."

Kyle watched Wren kneel beside Vestie's chair. "Zettie knows," she said softly. The grieving woman swiveled slightly toward Wren and mouthed silently, "Everthin'?" When Wren nodded Vestie bowed her head and sobbed silently. Her thick braid fell forward over her breast, exposing a slender, tanned neck so vulnerable Kyle was again reminded of a deer. But not one free in the wild. Rather he remembered one he'd seen caught in a trap, hobbled, and wounded, at the mercy of dogs closing in.

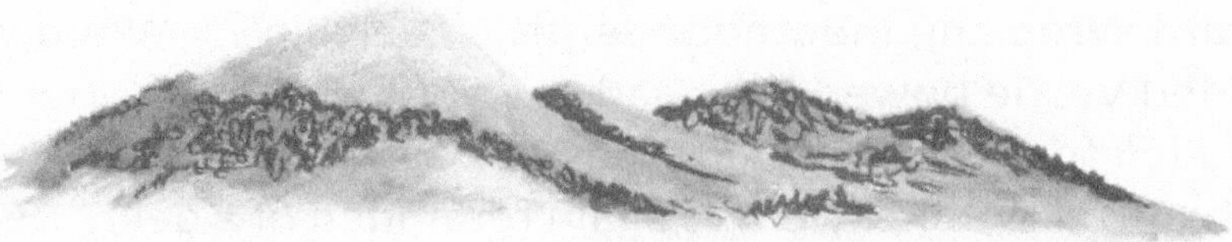

CHAPTER TWO

Wren, finding herself in the circle of women that enclosed Vestie, marveled how tragedy could break down walls that, under the ordinary rules of the mountain, could never be breached. She was suddenly and irrevocably one of them! Maudie subtly confirmed this by patting Wren's back and murmuring softly, "I went to school with Della, your Maw. There's lotsa' things I can tell you about her... not right now though. We've got a funeral to set up," she said with so much relish that Wren almost grinned despite herself. Trust the mountain folks to make an Event out of every occasion. Funerals were high on the list of mandatory celebrations. She could almost see Maudie's brain ticking off the numbers expected; the food required; the appropriate hymns....

Wren bestirred herself and set aside the question of how much the other women had overheard of the "private" conversation between the Glenning family and the Makepeace's. If she didn't do something soon, the planning of the memorial for Porter would be taken from Vestie and her children. Conversations reaching her from the kitchen about who would bring what and how soon should the church service be held made her realize that these women, in their kindly way, felt obliged to take over largely because they didn't believe Vestie capable.

Wren strongly disputed this assumption that Vestie was slow-witted, a belief that Porter had fostered through the years by his dismissive treatment of her.

"Vestie," Wren began, "there's a lot of folks here who want to help you. Are you ready to see to a few things?"

The blank, slightly surprised look Vestie gave Wren struck deep into Wren's heart and she felt suddenly like a lioness protecting her cub. But Vestie was no kitten and the sooner she showed it, the better it would be for all concerned. How to provoke her to action; to genuinely waken her? Escape into music wasn't an option right now. Wren grabbed Vestie's wrists, lifting her hands from the murmuring strings. Delphie's mewl of protest jerked Vestie out of her reverie.

"Vestie?" Wren peered deeply into her dark blue eyes and was rewarded with a flicker of interest. "Vestie? Maudie here wants to know – should they stay now and go on with the doin's or do you want them to leave?"

Vestie mutely studied the rag rug. When Wren continued to stare at her expectantly she struggled briefly to free her hands and irritation flashed in her eyes. Maudie had just opened her mouth to tell Cenia and Norie where to put the deviled eggs when Vestie turned and addressed her. "How … how many folks is here, do you think?"

"Jest the usual, honey," Maudie responded comfortingly. "We kin handle'em. You kin jest set there and be quiet-like."

When Vestie slanted a questioning glance at Wren who still held her wrists, Wren shook her head ever so slightly. Then she handed the dulcimer to Delphie and told her to put it up. Vestie stood up slowly but gracefully, tucking some stray hairs back behind her ear.

"Maudie," she said, sounding surprised at herself for addressing this formidable lady as an equal, "Maudie, I'd be obliged if you'ns would give me and Wren here some time to study on this. This is a family affair."

As startled as if the family cat had spoken, Maudie backed off, rubbing her hands across her ample bosom.

"Why shore, honey. Things kin wait a bit," she added doubtfully as she left the sun parlor trailed by the other women, now silent and mystified.

Wren, struck dumb herself by Vestie's inclusion of herself as family, watched them re-enter the kitchen, whispers and questions flying among them. Maudie stood at their center, much pleased to be the first to explain the Glenning family's new addition. Wren wondered what spin Maudie would put on her place in the family and how explain that Wren had only been "found" thirty-some years after Della's disappearance.

Vestie crossed the sun room and stared through a window at the men and women milling about in the grassy yard.

"So he's gone," she said quietly, her tongue slowly licking her pale lips. Vestie's shoulders seemed to lift as she turned back into the room. Wren rose from her position by the rocker to face the taller woman, her aunt-by-marriage. Shock and fear mingled in Vestie's eyes and her chin quivered slightly.

"What do you think, Wren? Should the folks all stay now? It won't be the party it was intended to be but mebbe, mebbe it'd be best to let'm talk it out here?"

"What do folks usually do when the news gets out that someone has died?" Wren asked.

Vestie's lips twitched, "Well, we'd generally go over to the house and take food and ....sometimes in the evenin' if it felt right, we might even sing some hymns. The women would help plan out the funeral and the men would figure out where the burial would be and if'n the hearse could make it up to the cemetery..." Vestie paused dreamily. "They had to take Granny Bureda's box out and carry her up on their shoulders. She passed jest afore Porter came a'courtin' me. It was the last funeral I was ever at," she reflected. "Generally Porter and the boys went to funerals and sech 'round here. I'd send over some pound cake or somethin'. But I din't go...." Vestie's voice trailed off and she wrinkled her brow as if wondering for the first time why this was so.

Wren's quick anger flared. This poor woman, not even allowed to attend a funeral? What was Porter about? What was he afraid of? Wren angrily slapped her hands on her jeans and Delphie jumped. She'd forgotten the silent child still standing by the dulcimer. Before she could apologize, Delphie flew across the room and out a side door. Through a window, Wren could see her streaking up the slope towards the woods.

"Let her go," Vestie said calmly. "She'll be okay."

Puzzled but willing to trust Vestie on this, Wren turned her mind back to the problems at hand. "Vestie, sounds like folks would gather anyway as soon as the news about Porter gets around. Why ask those already here to leave?" Even as she spoke, a dusty sheriff's vehicle turned into the barnyard. Apparently one of the men had radioed the patrol car. At Hershall or Denver's instigation? She doubted that Kyle or Locke would have bothered the law about Porter's death. Then again, maybe the officer was a family friend and was just stopping by to pay respects.

As other cars and trucks followed the cruiser in a steady procession, Wren marveled at the efficiency of the police scanner as the local purveyor of news and disasters. "Seems like everyone was tuned in this afternoon," Wren remarked, pointing to the crowd of folks converging on the porch.

Vestie peered out the window and jerked back. "What kin I do? All these folks ..." She wrapped her arms tightly around herself and rocked from side to side. Observing her, some of Wren's doubts returned. Vestie's eyes were closed but Wren keenly remembered her sharp, probing gaze when they'd related the facts about Porter's death.

"No," Wren reasoned, "Vestie's not dumb. Except perhaps in believing she deserved the treatment Porter handed out to her."

Once again Wren felt anger boiling up inside. What could she do? Vestie was family to her now and she'd be damned if she'd let Vestie be treated like that *again* ... by anyone, no matter how kindly. How could she begin to undo the damage Porter had done to this beautiful woman?

Crossing the room, Wren touched Vestie lightly on the elbow. "Vestie! Get hold of yourself. You've got a job to do!"

Vestie opened her eyes. "You sound jest like Grannie."

"Do I?" Wren queried.

Vestie nodded, "Only she'd say, "Git on with it, little gal. Ain't nobody in the world need face you down 'lessin' you let'm."

"Your Grannie was right, Vestie," Wren responded warmly, encouraged by these gritty words. "What would she expect you to do right now?"

"Why, she'd be tellin' me that those folks out there need tendin' to," Vestie said slowly, startled by her own admission. "She'd allas be the firstn' to a death and the last to leave. I took her plenty of times once she got so's she didn't drive herself." Wren watched Vestie square her shoulders and straighten up to her graceful height. Her eyes, though, mirrored Delphie's shyness and Wren still feared she might bolt for nearest hidey-hole.

"Vestie?" Wren repeated sharply and nodded toward the door. Folks were pushing into the front room. To Wren's relief, Vestie didn't slump back but walked reluctantly toward the gathering crowd as if she felt her Grannie's hand firmly at her back.

"Good for you, Grannie," Wren murmured to herself as she slipped out the side door to search for Kyle. She found him at the edge of a ring of men standing about the sheriff, who was questioning Porter's sons. The boys were angry, excited, and unaware of tears smudging their young faces. The grizzled sheriff listened gravely as they pushed their case for a fully mounted search for their father in the wilds of Unaka Mountain.

Wren raised her eyebrows at Kyle. "Not to worry, Wren," he said softly. "Sheriff Foch is not about to do anything. He already knows about the rock slide from the forest service folks and he's satisfied with their account of the lightning having set off the dynamite. Besides, do you think *he'd* want to go tramping up a mountain?" Kyle gestured toward the man whose beer belly hung several soft inches over the belt of his holster. "He's got enough problems just getting in and out of the squad car..."

"...or on and off a bar stool," Wren added to herself, as she studied the law officer, respected throughout the county for his protection of the locals whenever possible. One story, widely circulated, concerned how he escorted a state drug officer past a cornfield with marijuana growing throughout. The sheriff pointed to a mountain peak in the far distance where "the best white lightnin" used to be distilled, launching into a long story about how folks transported it out of Blackburne County in everything from coke bottles to five gallon jugs.

That evening, the teens responsible for the illegal (corn) crop, got a phone call instructing them that the cornfield had to be "weeded" by dawn when a helicopter survey of the county was scheduled.

The tendency of folks to take matters into their own hands rather than call in the law lifted some of the burden of his office from Sheriff Foch's shoulders. His deputies ... and they were legion ... did little more than collect their stipends while waiting outside homes where domestic quarrels had been reported by concerned neighbors.

Not even gunshots, *especially* gunshots, induced them to intervene before it was clear that the parties involved had effectively settled the matter under dispute. Wren occasionally wondered about the number of preventable deaths that had taken place during her years in Laurel Spring.

The sheriff cleared his throat and spat out a long stream of tobacco juice from the wad he'd been nursing in his jaw while the boys shouted their demands. "Now let's git the straight of it here, boys. You sayin' you don't think your Paw is dead? Or you sayin' there was foul play on account of yore Uncle Locke bein' on the scene and not savin' him?" He turned a sharp eye on the hefty man who was standing silently behind his nephews.

Before the boys could reply, a neatly dressed man in a button-down plaid shirt pushed into the crowd. "Pastor Arlas," the sheriff acknowledged gratefully. "These here boys are almighty upset. Might be you could talk some sense into 'em."

Pastor Arlas put his arms across the shoulders of the gangly boys, easily steering them toward the house by dint of his own stringy height. To Wren, his eyes looked cold for a man of the cloth but apparently Hershall and Denver Ray had enough respect for him not to resist his taking charge.

When the three of them reached the porch, Wren tugged on Kyle's arm. "I'm worried about Vestie," she began and explained the scene in the sun parlor after he and Locke had left.

Kyle listened thoughtfully and nodded. "We'll look in on her then but if she's doing okay, we've got to leave and get back to Laurel Spring. Remember, Mencie told us that old Gaither had something important to tell us, something so important she wouldn't even let you say good-by to Mamaw Zettie."

Wren frowned. She *had* forgotten. Family concerns had been front and center in her mind since they'd jumped into Kyle's truck at the trail's end.

"Family concerns," Wren thought and smiled wryly. She now had a family and despite the heaviness weighing on her,

Wren's heart warmed. She followed Kyle back into the front room of the large house and was pleased to find Vestie gamely facing the folks who milled around her. Pastor Arlas appeared to be riding herd on the boys for the moment and the women in the kitchen were efficiently passing out coffee, cold drinks and liberal plates of food.

"No need for me here," Wren murmured to Kyle, grateful she could now drive home to Laurel Spring. The prospect of some quiet time was powerfully alluring but she knew it would have to wait. Gaither would come first.

"We'll check in on Vestie here tomorrow," Kyle assured her.

Wren was turning her Civic around, when she glimpsed some movement at the edge of the woods behind the barn. Sun glinted briefly on a tangle of light curls. "Delphie! A little wild child," Wren reflected, her heart going out to this half-sister.

She waved and Delphie seemed to signal back. But then the child melted into the shadows of the woods. Had Delphie been watching for her? Should she follow the child? Wren's foot hovered uncertainly over the gas pedal but finally she opted to drive on toward Laurel Spring and whatever Ol' Gaither had to tell them. As she steered slowly over Panther Ridge, Wren was haunted by a sense that her kinship with Delphie ran deeper than blood.

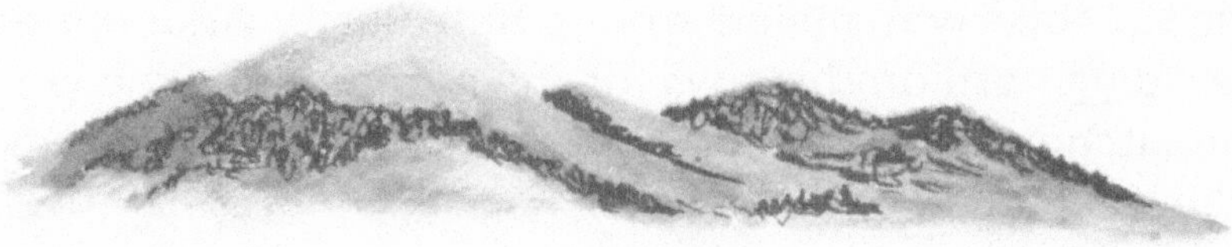

CHAPTER THREE

Arriving in town from the Glenning farm, Kyle had found Gaither leaning against the large window of the post office. The leather-skinned mountain man, pipe clenched between his five remaining teeth, had a large canvas bag at his feet into which he had stuffed papers, cans and other litter from the edge of Main Street. Gaither served the town as a self-appointed clean-up crew of one, making the rounds of "downtown" Laurel Spring (all three blocks) in all seasons and weathers.

Most people considered Gaither just another of the dim-witted characters who wandered the streets of a town where inbreeding had produced a striking percentage of "peculiar" people. Kyle himself had paid scant attention to this town fixture until a few weeks earlier when Gaither had hinted that he knew a way to Lovada Cove.

Mencie had literally barred their return to Zettie's house after their hike to Lovada Spring, telling Wren and Kyle about an urgent message that had come in from (of all people!) ol' Gaither. They were to look him up as soon as they reached Laurel Spring. Wren, however, had argued that they should first tell the Glenning family about Porter's death before meeting with Gaither. Kyle agreed, in part to be a support to Locke.

Once Kyle pulled up beside the post office, Gaither had waved a hand toward a grassy slope that had pretensions of being a park. Wren parked behind Kyle's truck and joined the two men as Gaither wandered along Turkey Creek, stabbing at trash. Kyle introduced Wren who had never actually spoken with Gaither despite waving at him daily for the past few years.

Though gaunt and dark with age, Gaither walked with vigor, scanning the ground swiftly, a black brimmed hat pulled low over his brow. When he looked up, Kyle noted his keen grey eyes, narrowed from years of surveying mountainous terrain. The slightly vacant smile that often curved Gaither's lips was replaced with a grim line.

"You'ns got the message, I take it," he began and Kyle was surprised at the authority in Gaither's voice.

"Mencie told us to look you up as soon as we got back," Kyle responded cautiously.

"That all she say?"

Kyle nodded, uncertain how much to admit. He couldn't yet gauge his standing with the Cove members who lived outside the community of elders in the Cove itself.

Gaither jabbed his stick through a paper snagged in the weeds and shucked it into his bag. Kyle recognized the swift moves of a hunter and, for the first time, wondered why this man of the woods spent his days patrolling the sad streets of a town shunned by all but those who had nowhere else to go. Half the stores were boarded up, the other half displayed dusty wares, some not seen for sale since the fifties.

Gaither pulled his pipe out of his mouth and peered at the cold bowl with distaste. "Folks have been a'tellin me some thangs that are mighty worrisome," he began. "Don' know how much youn's have seen fer yerselves...."

The older man studied the couple coolly, reminding Kyle again that they were outsiders in a community suspicious of all but its own. Wren shifted uncomfortably before crunching down on a beer can to add to Gather's collection.

Gaither nodded approvingly. Plucking a scrap of paper from his sack, he asked, "See this here? It's a label from a powdered milk box wrote up in English and Spanish. I see 'em all the time now."

Kyle frowned, uncertain where the old man was going. "It's on account of there's more and more Hispanics workin' round here in the 'bacca and t'mater fields," Gaither continued, as he expertly swished a bundle of oily rags bobbing in the creek to shore. "They tend to stay out of sight but they're here all right and its beginin' to look like a fair number aim to stay."

"Some of the younger men are turning up at the classes at the Center," Kyle observed.

"Them's the braver ones, I reckon," Gaither admitted and something in his tone jangled Kyle's alarms. He glanced over at Wren whose shoulders were tensed and waiting.

"Air's folks round here that don' want them brown folks to feel welcome," Gaither continued, as he mashed fresh tobacco into his pipe. He struck a match and clamped the shank between his teeth.

"Air's trouble brewin' and some of those who should be facin' it down are stirrin' it up." Gaither's eyes bored into Kyle. "You seen what I'm talking at?"

Kyle nodded reluctantly. A nasty situation was shaping up, one he'd hoped to ignore but doubted he'd have that luxury any longer.

"So what's turning so crucial right now?" he asked.

"It's comin' on summer and migrants are movin' up to work the fields. This year a number of the workers are bringin' their families with them which means they won't be bunkin' out by the fields but will be lookin' fer more decent places to live. There's been some meetin's a'ready and fellers are gittin' hot under the collar, not wantin' them folks livin' round their own families. Bad thing is, some of the pastors are aiggin' them on."

"And?" Kyle waited, knowing he hadn't heard the nub of the problem yet.

"Well, our folks are tryin' to calm things down and they're gettin' set upon. Now that's not new nor even so bad," Gaither admitted and spat on the ground.

"The trouble is, some of the pastors have got together and are pickin' out our people (they attend in all the church's here abouts). Some of the sharper preachers are beginnin' to figure out who's supportin' who and it looks like they might start exposin' some of our people as belongin' to a kind of sect or whatever...."

Gaither beat his dusty hat on his leg, causing Wren to step back from a rising cloud to avoid a sneezing fit. She frowned as Gaither continued.

"You two know that Cove members don' need to be picked out, or picked *on*, as fer as thet goes. We ain't all that different or better'n other folks but we try to hold to what is right and good. And we cain't back down from it."

"So where do we come in?" Kyle asked.

"Cause youn's are new here, no one's goin' to tie you to The Cove. You got to be the ones to rally the good folks in this county – our people will be among'em but they cain't be seen as leaders. They's plenty of folk that kin be swayed one way or ta'other, at this point. We got to act afore somethin' really turrible comes down the pike." Gaither threw Kyle and Wren a look so hard they almost ducked.

Kyle took a deep breath and let his eyes wander over the mountainous slopes surrounding Laurel Spring. "Ironic," he thought, that this little town sat in an ancient volcanic caldera. Although quiescent since time beyond memory, hot, muddy springs still broke through here and there in the bowl-like valley where spring bloomed early and leaves turned late.

In past centuries, this area had been regarded as holy ground for all the native tribes living along the east coast. No warrior could carry weapons or attack an enemy within the sacred vale. Everyone had safe access to the healing waters. Ignored since the 1920's, there was recent talk of advertising these naturally restorative waters and piping them into a pool or hot tubs.

Kyle Gray Wolf Makepeace, wearer of the mantle of a shaman of his tribe, continued to stare into the distance, hearing many voices echo behind the words of Old Gaither. His own secret name, Echota, which his father had bestowed on him at the bedside of his dying twin, was an ancient town of refuge in the heart of the Smokies and once the capital of the Tsalagi (Cherokee) nation.

That town had been destroyed during the struggles leading up to the brutal relocation of the Cherokee people in 1839, a trek now known as the Trail of Tears. Kyle's ancestors were among the families that had avoided the round-up by fleeing deep into the ridges and ravines of their mountain homeland. These survivors now formed the Eastern Band of the Cherokee.

When Kyle had chosen to live in Laurel Spring, he knew it was a place of healing but he had initially settled there with defiance in his heart. That anger had been literally overthrown through his recent experiences at Lovada Spring. Was he now being given a mandate to unite the current population, mainly Scots-Irish, with the sacred mysteries of this land, the power of which they were largely unaware?

Laurel Spring could become a new town of refuge, a place of acceptance and healing for many rejected souls. Much as Kyle wished it otherwise, he knew he could not again walk away from his calling.

Wren's sudden sneeze woke Kyle from his reverie. His gaze returned to Gaither who had been observing him intently. Those grey eyes seemed to reflect full knowledge of who Kyle was and was called to become. He also noted profound compassion on Ol' Gaither's face.

Kyle felt Wren move closer to him. She rested her hand on his arm, lightly indicating her understanding of the pain that underlay his frequent and familiar lapses into the past. Slowly Kyle swept the panorama of the mountains surrounding them, begging for a share in their strength and nobility.

With his hand covering the medicine pouch concealed beneath his shirt, Kyle nodded formal acceptance to Gaither. What the future held, he could not fathom. All he perceived was the current task laid upon him.

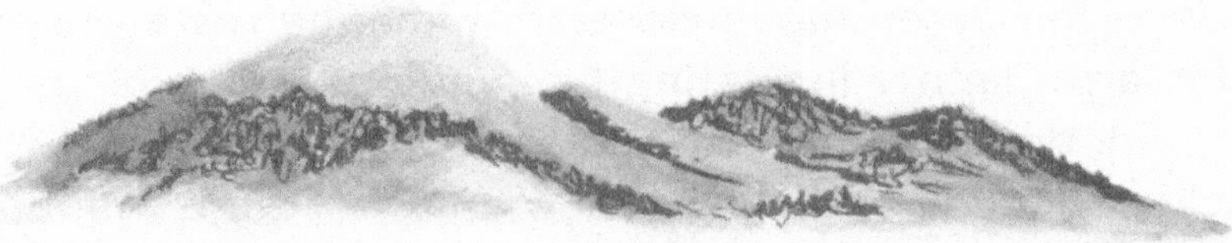

CHAPTER FOUR

Cautiously Kyle shifted his tail bone from a discomforting intimacy with the walnut pew of Panther United Brethren church (PUB, for short) and continued his study of the ceiling fan turning lazily above Pastor Arlas' head. Amazing how the colored light from the stained glass window in the sanctuary glittered on its blades and then bounced off the preacher's bald spot with every bob of his head. It reminded Kyle of a disco he had once frequented ...even the preacher's mesmeric pounding on the pulpit simulated the drumming of a most forgettable rock band. A sharp pain in his ribs startled Kyle and Wren hissed into his ear, "Kyle Makepeace, don't you dare start laughing ..."

Crossing his arms across his chest, Kyle tried to distract himself from the growing farce the preacher was making of Porter Glenning: a fearless hunter, patriotic leader, enlightened educator, God-fearing Christian, provident husband, loving father, upright defender of the rights of women, children, dogs... dogs? The rhythmic drumming beat on.

"I wonder where (if?) Pastor Arlas studied homiletics...or even Scripture," Kyle mused, as the preacher forged on in full cry, describing the Almighty Judge driving his sheep into heavenly mansions (Porter in the lead) while the goats dove

into hell and the stars and stripes flew forever.

After a dramatic pause, during which the rafters continued to vibrate, Pastor Arlas sucked in a deep breath and choked violently. Despite a secret hope that this presaged a fatal attack, Kyle nevertheless joined several other men rushing toward the pulpit where the purple-faced orator swayed. Doc Tanner reached the stricken man first and with what seemed to Kyle unnecessary vigor, performed the Heimlich maneuver which dislodged a large horse fly from the pastor's windpipe.

Before the stricken orator could be fully restored to his pulpit, the organist burst into a triumphant chorus of "Leaning on the Everlasting Arms" and the church elders bore their limp pastor down the aisle in place of a rolling casket. The congregation gratefully spilled out of the sweltering church into the June sunlight.

Lacking a body to bury, the funeral cortege wound its way directly over Panther Ridge to the Glenning farm where a dinner of baked ham, deviled eggs, mustard greens and vast quantities of soup beans awaited the mourners. From their position near the head of the procession, Wren twisted around in the cab of Kyle's pickup and tried to count the vehicles following them. "Looks like most of the county turned out," she observed.

"A funeral brings folks out from every cove and holler," Kyle responded, impressed himself by the number of vehicles that were filing out of the parking lot behind Panther United Brethren. "I just hope they all left their guns at home," he added darkly, aware of the many clans and cliques that made up Blackburne County.

"Well, the Glenning boys certainly didn't," Wren observed, pointing to the loaded gun rack in the back window of the truck immediately ahead of them. Hershall Lincoln and Denver Ray were crouched behind their mother and Locke in the king cab of the black pick-up. To judge by Locke's stony face and the angry gestures from the boys, a family feud was in progress. Vestie stared out the side window, appearing oblivious to the tensions swirling around her.

Kyle nodded in her direction. "I wonder what it will take to waken that woman?"

"So do I," Wren responded grimly. She had told Kyle of her disappointment that, despite her urging, Vestie had allowed the neighbors and Pastor Arlas to plan her husband's memorial service. Vestie had immersed herself in the familiar rhythms of the farm but showed no interest in arranging the memorial service for her husband.

Wren could sympathize with Vestie's apathy for she knew she had little reason to mourn Porter's death. Kyle, too, doubted that it was grief that immobilized Vestie. *Was* she as slow as Porter had led others to believe? Or had Porter so profoundly humiliated her that Vestie was a hopelessly broken woman?

Wren had angrily reported to Kyle that the boys, imitating their father, treated their mother like a servant, someone capable of little more than cooking, cleaning and chopping tobacco. Only Delphie, in her wordless, loving way related to Vestie as a person.

The sole times Vestie seemed to be fully alive was when she was playing her dulcimer or singing. Even now, Wren recalled hearing her humming softly *"There is a Balm in Gilead"* as she went about her household chores and baking bread for the meal that would follow Porter's Memorial.

Wren remembered with chills, the morning she drove into the Glenning place and heard Vestie belting out an old version of *Barbary Allen* as she hung out a line-full of denim jeans, bib overalls, and work shirts. Birds twittered a descant in the background and Delphie, sitting on an upturned wash tub, swayed to the rhythm. It was Wren's first clue that Delphie was not deaf. The child never spoke but Wren began to suspect that she understood everything said around her – and quite possibly, a good deal that was not said. Wren told Kyle her belief that both mother and daughter may have used the "slowness" attributed to them as a shield against abuse from Porter and the boys.

Watching the angry gestures in the vehicle ahead of them, Kyle's hands twitched on his steering wheel. He longed to knock some sense into those arrogant young pups. Locke had barely braked the truck when Kyle saw Hershall and Denver Ray explode angrily out the side doors and head for the barn.

Apparently Locke had been trying to do just what Kyle recommended and the "pups" were having none of it. Kyle's mind was further disturbed as he watched Vestie drift toward the house, pausing to sniff the roses climbing over the arbor near the back door. Something was definitely wrong with this scene. Suddenly he missed Delphie. Where was the child? Why had she not attended the service for her father?

"Wren," Kyle asked sharply, "where's Delphie?"

Wren had slipped from her seat, awkwardly shifting a pan of coleslaw from her lap to her arms. Quickly scanning the yard, she waved towards the woods beyond the house. "She's up there."

Kyle turned and caught a glimpse of movement among some blossoming briar bushes. A small shape was slipping deeper into the shadows. He frowned and pulled at his nose. "How did you know Delphie was there, Wren?"

Wren paused by the steps to the kitchen door, hugging the pan against her chest, startled by his question. "Well, I just did, I guess" she said, adding slowly. "How can I *not* know where she is?"

Kyle felt the hairs on his neck stand up. "Wren? What did you just say? That you just *know* wherever Delphie is? Doesn't that strike you as strange? Until last week, you didn't even know she existed."

"No," Wren spoke slowly, softly, "I didn't...yet I've always known of her." She shivered and looked up at Kyle, her eyes both puzzled and scared.

"Vestie told me something a few days ago. Seems just after Delphie was born, both Mamaw Zettie and Mencie turned up and insisted that Vestie name the baby, Della, after Porter's missing sister. Apparently Porter was so incensed by their interference, he actually grabbed his rifle but Mencie faced him down by mentioning his "other" daughter. Porter had stormed out of the house and from then on, acted as if Delphie did not exist. It was the first hint Vestie had that Porter had fathered a child before he'd married her."

"Does Vestie know that Della was your mother?" Kyle asked softly.

"Yes, she understands that now," Wren responded. "And she doesn't seem to be as horrified as I was. Zettie hurts, of course." Wren paused, a profound sadness overshadowing her face. "I suspect that's why they settled on calling her Delphie."

Kyle turned Wren around gently until she was looking directly into his eyes. "Do you know how much Delphie favors you? From the pictures I've seen of you at her age, you could've passed for twins." Wren smiled faintly, "We had the same father, did we not? She's my half-sister after all."

Kyle nodded, realizing that Wren had already given much thought to her relationship with Vestie's mute daughter. That it would eventually involve him, Kyle had little doubt. Just now he was curious about Vestie's feelings towards both of Porter's rejected daughters.

"How does Vestie regard Delphie?" he asked softly.

Wren pondered. "I think Vestie believes Delphie has... gifts and is "warded by the spirits", as she puts it. She told me that Mencie had cradled Delphie in her arms for a long time, just studying her. When she gave the baby back to Vestie, Mencie had warned her not to worry if Delphie developed a bit of a wild streak. She would need it when her time came."

Kyle felt a rush of apprehension for he recognized the biblical allusion in Mencie's words. Who or what was Delphie? Was she merely a mute of limited intelligence or...

"Wren," Kyle grabbed his wife's arm anxiously, "What do those words mean to you?"

"I'm not sure," Wren responded slowly. "I fear for Delphie. But from what Vestie told me of Mencie's reaction to the baby, Mencie not only fears *for* Delphie but fears the child herself; almost as if Delphie has some power Mencie dreads ...though what *Mencie* could possibly fear, I have no notion."

Kyle shared Wren's confusion about Delphie. He suspected that this strange Innocent could be either dangerous or salvific, like a two-edged sword. There were legends among his people about wisdom teachers who appeared at appropriate times to refocus people on paths of harmony, courses on which the preservation of the universe could depend.

The teachers on the Qualla Boundary where his Cherokee relatives lived were saying the times were right for another such wisdom figure to arise, one who would be a teacher of great compassion, one who would rekindle the wisdom fire of right relations among all creatures. Delphie no doubt had some Cherokee blood in her, as did most of the folks in these mountains. Could *she* be the one?

Lost in speculation, Kyle had forgotten they still stood on the path to the Glenning's back door until Wren touched him lightly. "Kyle, we need to explore this more but right now the ladies are waiting for this coleslaw. It'll have to be later, okay?" She lifted the pan she was cradling, smiling ruefully.

As if on cue, Maudie called through the screen door. "Wren, honey! Bring that slaw in here afore it curdles and help me to git these biscuits agoin'." Wren eagerly mounted the back steps and merged into the crowd of chattering women in the kitchen.

Kyle turned away, smiling to himself for he knew how it thrilled his little wife to find herself included in the closed social circle of these mountain women. He headed toward the barn where he had spotted some men gathering in the shade around a cooler. A cold one would be mighty welcome right now.

Strolling toward the barn, Kyle overheard Creed roughly questioning Hershall and Denver Ray. "What do you mean, boys? You tellin' us that Locke is plannin' to use Mexican hands in *your* bacca fields? Ain't no reason why youn's can't do it yourselves. Your Maw there's a strong woman."

Hershall and Denver Ray nodded vigorously. "'at's what *we* said, Creed," Hershall fumed. "But Uncle Locke, he ain't listenin' to us. He's treatin' us like we was kids ... like this ain't our place."

A couple of other men shook their heads. "Don't let him do that to you, boys," Woots said sympathetically. "Bad enough that you've done lost your Pa in that accident...leastways that's what Locke calls it. Now he's tryin' to take over your farm?" Woots shifted his thin shoulders under his shirt, his sharp nose twitching like a weasel's.

Denver sniffled and wiped the back of his hand across his eyes. Creed patted his back kindly. "You boys have seen enough bad luck. You don't need no workers from down south messin' 'round your place. They ain't even Christian, son. They're most of 'em Catlics. Ain't that right, Pastor Arlas?"

The skinny preacher waved an empty beer bottle at Creed. "Now we can't go puttin' folks down, Creed, on account of their upbringin'. It's true I wouldn't let a one of'em cross the threshold of Panther United Brethren, still belongin' to the devil 'cause they ain't been baptized proper."

"Devil worshipers, you think, Pastor?" Woots asked eagerly, his thin tongue darting round his lips.

"Woots Gander, that's a mighty heavy charge. I didn't say any such thing," Pastor Arlas declared as he accepted another bottle from Creed and winked. "And you don' say nothin' 'bout how this here bottle got into my hand, understand, boys?" Creed's bushy black moustache bristled as he grinned.

As Kyle reached into the cooler, he studied the faces of the men gathered around Pastor Arlas and the Glenning boys. He did not like what he saw. It reminded him of what he'd seen in films made in Selma, Alabama during the sixties. Then it was blacks; now it was Hispanics.

During the six years he'd lived in Blackburne County, Kyle had seldom seen any migrant workers (nor blacks either, come to think of it) shopping in Laurel Spring or eating at the local diner. So far as he knew, no Hispanic families lived in Blackburne County though neighboring counties had their share.

Liston, a burly bearded man, pushed into the group. "Preacher Kanardy over at the Methodist church don't have much use for 'em neither, not since he caught one of their boys lookin' to rob the Relief Fund. We was taking up a collection for Granny Dawson's boy who was jest gettin' out of prison down in Raleigh and needed money to git back to home."

"Wonder how they know'd about that collection?" Woots mused, his nose twitching. "Makes a person think, don't it?"

"Think what, Woots?" Iverson challenged as he hitched up his jeans. "Them boys weren't doin' nothin' but walkin' past the church when services let out, so I heard. You fellers seem to be almighty fast with this kind of insinuatin' talk. If'n there's anything suspicious round here, I'd look to *you* afore I'd lay it on folks we don't know nothin' about!"

"That's jest it, Ive," Hershall shouted, "We don't know *nothin'* about these folks."

"'Ceptin' their gurls is mighty purty, ain't they, Hersh?" Denver teased. "Yeh, man, the little dark-haired gal that Hersh tried to pick up ain't a patch on any one of the gals from around here. 'Course, she took one look at Hersh here, and was gone so fast, he's still wonderin' if she jest plumb disappeared into thin air. Bein' as drunk as a skunk that night, he might've jest passed out and made up the rest..."

Denver's voice suddenly broke thanks to a body blow delivered by his red-faced brother. Although Kyle welcomed the shift of focus, he didn't want to see Vestie further humiliated by her boys sparring at their father's memorial service.

Before the other men could urge the brothers on, Kyle thrust his stocky body between the riled boys and grabbed Hershall's arm. "Drop it, son," he grunted, and shook the boy's wrist sharply until a skinning knife clattered to the dirt.

At the same time, Iverson pinioned Denver's arms behind his back. "He pulled a knife on me!" Denver spluttered. "Let me at 'im!"

Kyle swung Hershall around to face him and looked deep into the boy's glassy eyes. "You young shit!" he exclaimed, "You're doing pot. You could've cut up your own brother bad in the state you're in!"

Suddenly Locke grabbed his nephew by the hair and dunked his face several times into the scummy watering trough conveniently at hand. When Locke finally turned the boy loose, he was spluttering and breathless. Locke stalked off wiping the filth from his hands. Hershall's lips were curled but silent.

Iverson released Denver who walked over to his older brother. To Kyle's surprise, the boy threw his arm around Hershall's shoulders and the two brothers ambled off towards the tables the women had set up under the trees by the house.

"Guess they feel like all they've got left is each other," Doc Tanner observed. Kyle nodded, grabbed a beer and headed back toward his truck. He needed time to think.

CHAPTER FIVE

Wiping her face with the hem of the borrowed apron she wore, Wren stood on the back steps of the Glenning kitchen and scanned the group of men for sight of her husband. A discussion among the women in the kitchen had grown hotter than the oven where she had been pulling out trays of golden brown biscuits. Wren had been assigned to monitoring the buns because she couldn't keep up with the mountain women who mixed and patted flour and lard into biscuits as speedily as they beat their gums over the latest gossip.

As the breeze dried the sweat on her face, Wren spotted Kyle leaning against their red pick-up, beer in hand. Doc Tanner had ambled over to him, a somber look on his round face. The two men were talking quietly as Wren moved in their direction.

"Am I interrupting something?" she asked coming around the bed of the truck.

"You are, Mam, but it's something I expect Kyle will fill you in about," Doc Tanner replied before Kyle could open his mouth. The vet gave her husband a knowing glance before asking Wren,

"My Maudie in the kitchen?"

"No, I think she's gone with Cenia and Norie to set up the desserts under the arbor," Wren replied with a smile. She liked Carson Tanner and his motherly wife, Maudie, who had been among the first to welcome her to Laurel Spring after she and Kyle were married.

The vet nodded toward Wren and strode toward the arbor, his body firm and well-muscled despite late middle age. Doc Tanner's work was mainly with large animals and he was as sun-darkened as the farmers who depended on his services.

Wren turned back to Kyle and noted the seriousness in his eyes. "What's up?" she asked.

"You remember our talk with Ol' Gaither last week, the day we got back from The Cove?"

Wren nodded. How could she forget it? As a result, she had resigned her position with Western Carolina University and was now engaged in a discouraging search for a job in Laurel Spring where she could be more directly involved with the community the Cove elders wanted them to serve.

"Carson was filling me in on a meeting he attended at Creed Handler's place last night," Kyle began. "Gaither's right about the bad feelings towards the Mexicans who are moving their families up here. The men that gathered at Creed's are determined to make it so ... um, "uncomfortable" for migrant workers that they'll be afraid to settle their women and children in Blackburne County."

Wren felt both shocked and sick at heart. Secretly she had hoped that Ole' Gaither was exaggerating the situation; that his anxiety was misplaced. But conversations she'd just overheard in the kitchen had made her realize that many of the women were genuinely afraid of the migrant workers and believed all the tales of stealing and rape that were circulating.

Norie Handler had loudly described how she'd warned her daughters against having anything to do with the young migrants who were working their tobacco fields this year.

"Who all were at the meeting?" Wren asked.

"Creed, Liston, Woots, Iverson and his son, Milt, Worth ... seems like most of the men from up around Panther Ridge here....

"And?" Wren prompted, sensing her husband was reluctant to tell her all he knew.

"Sheriff Foch was there."

"Why am I not surprised?" Wren murmured wryly. "Who else, Kyle?"

Kyle took a deep breath. "Pastor Arlas was there, as well as Kanardy, the preacher from near Laurel Spring. Couple of other church leaders as well – the deacon from the Baptist church near Viney Branch and Father Bill Daws from Prince of Peace in Laurel Spring."

Wren felt perspiration break out on her face. It sounded like the whole of Blackburne County was being caught up in this. "So, tell me what happened," she asked, her throat dry and stiff.

"Carson said it got pretty rowdy 'cause not everyone there agreed what should be done… or if anything need be done." Kyle paused, pulling on his nose as he pondered all he'd heard. "I think Doc was trying to calm things down; to get the men to think things through before they did something they'd regret later."

"Such as?"

"He didn't want to tell me. He's protecting his neighbors … and trying to protect the Mexicans at the same time." Kyle shook his head. "I wonder just how long Carson can straddle the issue, not coming down on either side. On one hand, he's been doing a bit of medical "advising" for the Hispanics as well as for their animals. Most of the Mexican women are afraid to bring their children into the Clinic in Laurel Spring."

Wren winced. "He could get into serious trouble doing that."

"He knows it but he's just too good-hearted not to help out where it's so plainly needed. I suspect he's also passed out some antibiotics and allergy pills that the folks couldn't get any other way."

"Wouldn't it be safer if he just brought them into the Clinic? Cenia mentioned that her boy, Milt, does that once in a while."

Kyle rubbed his nose and frowned, "Doc's not the kind of man to alienate friends. And he'd be sure to have Creed and his crowd down on him if anyone caught him doing that."

"He's going to have the law down on him if it gets out that he's treating people as well as their animals," Wren snapped, worry creasing her forehead. "and if Sheriff Foch was at the meeting ....

"What sort of lawman is he? I used to wonder why no one checked out the vans that often go by our place at night. Everyone *knows* that illegal aliens are being transported through our county." Wren had heard a heartbreaking account of an accident where a dozen migrants had been found injured or killed while locked in the back of an unmarked vehicle – a truck from which the driver had disappeared.

Wren grabbed Kyle's arm anxiously. "Kyle, I have to tell you something I just overheard in the kitchen. Some of the women were talking with Norie, Creed's wife. She overheard her girls, Beckie and Lisa, whispering about something. Hershall Glenning had come over to see Beckie last night and when he noticed the men gathering in the barn, he'd snuck around back and climbed up into the loft. Apparently he was boasting to Beckie and Lisa later about doing something to drive the Mexicans out of Blackburne County real soon."

Kyle's eyes narrowed. "Those boys are so full of hurt and anger right now there's no telling what damn fool thing they might try."

Wren nodded. "And Vestie doesn't seem to even care what they do. She's still wandering around in a fog not able to figure out a thing for herself – like she's still afraid Porter will come back. She's not slow by any means but she's lost all sense of her own strength; her own value." Wren paused and then added thoughtfully, "Seems like Porter's ruined her just as badly as he did my mother."

"He did that," Kyle agreed, "and he taught his boys to regard Vestie merely as a servant. There's no way she could stop Hershall or Denver Ray even if she knew what they were up to. And they're so angry at Locke, they'd be sure to do exactly what he warned them *against*."

"It's a bad scene all the way around," Wren murmured, as she brushed her short reddish hair off her sweaty forehead. "I'm hoping that it will help Vestie to believe Porter's really gone when we all go back to The Cove and mark where he's buried by the rock slide. Locke's planning to take us in next week."

"Let's hope it will, Wren," Kyle said. Wren heard the doubt in Kyle's voice and was about to question him when she heard some screaming over near the picnic tables. Were the women wailing or laughing? She dashed around the vehicles parked near the barn with Kyle on her heels.

From a distance, she could see Maudie rocking back and forth on a bench, arms wrapped across her ample bosom and tears of laughter streaming down her face. Cenia was standing near her, breathless and hysterical, as they both watched Norie who was telling them a story in which Creed seemed to figure prominently. She gestured graphically with a slice of watermelon, describing how Creed, trying to bundle tobacco leaves for drying, got wrapped in the rope along with the tobacco.

Despite his hollering like a stuck pig, the girls had hauled him along with the tobacco, up to the rafters of the barn where the button on his jeans flew off and his pants ... his pants just sort of slid down... By then, Norie choked on her laughter but the picture was clear.

Pink juice trickled off Maudie's double chin and Cenia was spitting watermelon seeds all over the table cloth. A couple other matrons were wandering around sucking on slices of cold melon and giggling like school girls.

Some of the children who had been playing nearby stopped their games, transfixed by the sight of their Maws and Mamaws staggering around the dessert table. Pastor Arlas' prune-faced wife, Marzelle, the terror of the Sunday school crowd, tripped over a tree root and landed abruptly on her skinny bottom, her flowered dress flying up in her face. This set off another round of hysterical laughter and when petite Miss Althea tried to help her up and instead, landed in her lap, the rest of the women collapsed on the ground beside them, laughing helplessly.

Wren's perplexity only increased when she heard Kyle exclaim behind her, "Oh, hell, we're in trouble. Where's Doc Tanner?"

Fortunately, Carson Tanner had heard the commotion and was rushing over, a number of stunned and disappointed men on his heels. Liston and Woots were shouting, "Damn you, Ive, how'd you let them wimmen git aholt of that there melon from the shed? We fergot about it the other day when we heerd about Porter but figured it'd be good fer this here funeral dinner."

Comprehension lit Wren's face when she caught a strong whiff of corn liquor rising from the watermelon and she whirled on Kyle.

"Don't tell me you knew about this?" He nodded sheepishly but ducked her quick hand.

"Hey, look at Vestie," he cried in a desperate attempt to divert his furious wife. Wren glanced over her shoulder and her mouth fell open. A pink-cheeked Vestie had grabbed up a fiddle and was sawing away, her slim figure swaying joyously.

As she watched, Maudie grabbed Cenia and before anyone knew it, the two women were on top of the picnic table, clogging and clapping. The children were delighted and before long many of them joined their Ma's, stamping and whooping on the tables and benches. Vestie's fiddling merged into a reel and Norie began calling a turkey-trot.

Wren was grinning despite herself, the more so, when she realized that the only glum faces around were those of the men ambling away dispiritedly. Glancing up at Kyle, she shrugged, snagged a slice of watermelon and joined the dancers. Most of the women knew what made this particular melon so "tasty" and gladly shared it among themselves, but wisely guarded it from any man foolish enough to meander close by the table.

Creed, his face dark with anger, came up behind his wife, Norie, and clapped a hand over her mouth. When the reel screeched to a halt, the rest of the women looked up. Before Creed realized he'd just made a serious tactical error, a dozen mountain women were advancing on him, feisty from liquor and all too willing to rally to Norie's side.

Wren stepped down from the bench where Beckie Handler had been teaching her to clog and studied the developing situation with great interest. She glanced over her shoulder and noted how Kyle with some other men were prudently disappearing in the direction of the barn. Creed was clearly on his own.

The unfortunate man began to back off when he realized he that he was not only alone but surrounded by an unbroken circle of high ladies. Vestie tossed back her braid, loosened in the heat, and gave the sweating man a steely glance. She waved her bow like a baton and one of the women – was it Miss Althea? – cried, "You go, girl!"

Tucking the fiddle under her chin, Vestie began a jig as foot–tapping and soul-stirring as any Wren had ever heard. The women encircling Creed slowly began advancing on him, clapping, stomping, and screaming like panthers on a scent. Just before they actually touched the trembling man, they grabbed hands and skipped backwards. The circle widened when Beckie and Lisa pulled Wren into the group. Laughing and screeching they advanced once more on the stocky farmer who was desperately searching for a chance to break through the linked arms and stomping feet.

Vestie's fiddle called the dancers into a swirling circle, heading first in one direction, then in the other. Seen from a distance, the women, some hefty, some skinny, still mostly clad in their funeral clothes, might have seemed ludicrous but for the fierce energy that Vestie's playing released in them. The other men, drawn back against their better judgment, reappeared from behind the barn and stood slack-jawed, fascinated by the transformation in their women.

Kyle, acting on an inspiration he could not explain, suddenly ran forward, linked his arm through Wren's, and danced her into the center of the circle. Other men followed his cue and soon the lawn was filled with whirling couples.

Before long, a few banjo pickers joined in and the dance went on. Locke appeared with his fiddle and took over Vestie's part as her arm faltered. Wren noted how his gaze followed Vestie as, flushed and bright-eyed, she accepted another slice of melon from Maudie.

The children had discovered the unguarded dinner table and food was disappearing at an alarming rate. The rest of the men dragged the beer cooler over near the table and fell on the ham, slaw and soup beans with gusto.

Porter's funeral had turned into a festival and no one seemed to mind except Denver Ray and Hershall who prowled sullenly around the edges of the crowd. As the long June evening slowly darkened, the music changed and gradually, singing replaced dancing.

Lanterns lit the musicians on the porch who rendered ballads requested by the folks sitting on benches or on blankets spread over the grass. Often people called for Vestie to sing some of the old ballads and she complied, her voice strong and sure. Wren counted herself lucky to be participating in this spontaneous songfest, aware that it was a rare, living tradition passed down through generations of mountain folk.

Despite her absorption in the music, Wren caught sight of a small shadow lurking just beyond the circle of light. Whispering briefly to Kyle, Wren slipped off the bench and went in search of Delphie whom she found under the lilac bush near the back door.

"Hungry, honey?" she asked softly and was pleased when Delphie scrambled up and slipped her hand into Wren's. The little girl quietly accompanied Wren to the ravaged picnic table and accepted the sandwich and soup beans Wren heaped onto a paper plate. Once the child was eating, Wren sat next to her, noticing a gleam in her eyes whenever Vestie sang.

Just as some folks started picking up their blankets to leave, Miss Althea called out, "Vestie dear, give us *"Beautiful River."* Others echoed the request and Vestie, who had been sitting to one side of the players, reached for her dulcimer. She strummed it delicately and silence settled over the group. Locke fit his fiddle to his shoulder and moved behind Vestie. She began to sing softly at first but encouraged by humming from the group, Vestie gradually raised her voice until it rang clearly across the hushed crowd.

Wren missed Delphie at her side and stretched her neck until she caught sight of the child slipping up onto the porch where her mother was singing. As if mesmerized, the little girl, her pale hair a nimbus in the soft lantern glow, drifted toward Vestie, swaying gently. Wren saw her mouth moving as Vestie sang out, "yes, we'll gather at the river, the beautiful, the beautiful river ..." and wondered if Delphie might even have a voice.

Before Wren could focus on that question, her mind was suddenly filled with the glorious memory of Lovada Spring, sparkling in the morning sun, when she and Kyle had seen it only a couple weeks earlier. The water had leapt up shining like the crystal tide of the old Gospel song. Only she, as Keeper of the Spring, could find the way to it, if and when she was required.

As if sensing Wren's vision, Delphie turned toward her. Mirrored in the child's doe-like eyes, Wren saw the implacable foresight of Mencie, ageless Warder of the Borderlands. So vivid was the impression that Wren wondered if Mencie herself was here at the Memorial. Who else would know the secret that Wren carried within her?

She shifted uncomfortably, deeply disturbed by a deluge of memories. But by the time she and Kyle were driving off Panther Ridge, Wren had pushed her concerns down to where she buried everything she wasn't ready to deal with. In the dark cab, lit only by the glow from the dash, Kyle didn't notice his wife's grim expression. He had been distracted by Hershall and Denver Ray's plundering of the beer cooler whenever they figured no one was watching.

Wren was startled when Kyle suddenly asked what she knew about Vestie's ability to control the boys. "She seems to be taken up more with Delphie than with the boys," he grumbled.

"True," Wren observed, her eyes on the road unfolding in their headlights. "I think she expects Locke to handle Hershall and Denver."

Kyle grunted. "I suspect he's too troubled by his feelings for Vestie to deal fairly with her boys. And they're not dumb. They can see which way the wind is blowing and are likely to take advantage of it."

Wren merely settled back into her seat, wanting nothing more at this moment than to forget she had any connection with the Glenning family.

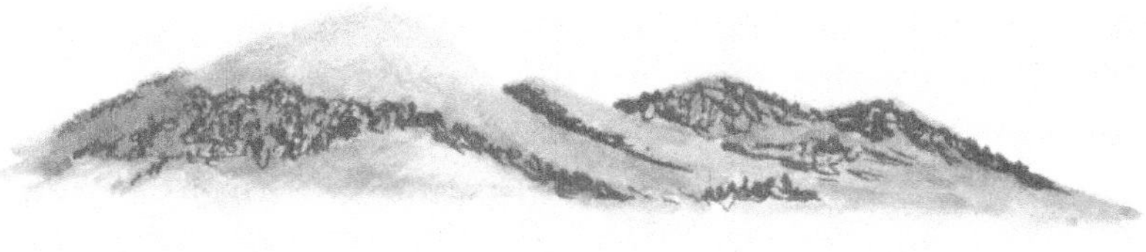

CHAPTER SIX

A week after the Memorial Service for Porter in Panther Gap, Wren and Kyle returned to The Cove with Locke, Vestie and the three youngsters. Along with Zettie, they went to the site of the rock slide where Porter had died. The boys were devastated when they saw the enormous rocks and heaps of debris dislodged by the dynamite blast. Whatever hope they'd clung to about their Pa escaping was brutally dashed.

Hershall stalked angrily over the devastated mountain-side, viciously hurling rocks at everything that moved. For once Denver didn't trail his older brother but stayed close to his Ma. He didn't even seem to mind Locke being near at hand, holding an umbrella over Mamaw Zettie's bent figure as a steady drizzle created rivulets in the raw mud.

In the misting dampness, Mencie ranged over the site seeking a sense of where Porter's body might be buried. In her grey poncho and drooping brimmed hat, she almost merged into the landscape. Once she had to dodge a rock that Hershall had sent flying at her feline familiar, The Dean. The large grey cat had fluffed out his fur, hissing angrily. He was still growling when Mencie turned back to the huddle of mourners with a worried look in her eyes. The ends of her long grey braids dripped as she lifted her hands apologetically.

"Ah'm walkin' in circles and kin feel him here abouts but restless-like, disturbed. It's like trying to find somethin' in a cave where the torch keeps blowin' out – the airs are all fretful. Ah've seen this afore when a person is not at rest. Ah hate to say this, Vestie, but yore man was open to dark spirits and they ain't quite left him yit."

Vestie sucked in her breath and seized Wren's arm. Wren nearly squealed as Vestie's strong fingers dug in convulsively but she recognized Vestie's panic. If Porter's spirit was still prowling, it could mean…? Gently Wren covered Vestie's hand with her own.

"Just wait, honey," Wren murmured. "He found forgiveness at the end. It just takes a while for a soul to accept it and be at peace."

Mencie waved at the gashed slope. "Ah suggest we jest give in and put the cross here, near where this little branch runs on down."

Vestie nodded numbly and vainly tried to beckon Hershall to join Denver Ray, and Delphie by her side. Finally Locke strode across the loose shale and grabbed Hershall's shoulder in order to steer him back to his waiting family. Mencie taking in the boy's bitter expression, shook her head. "Tain't good," she mouthed to herself.

Somehow, they stumbled through a few prayers before Kyle and Locke took turns with a posthole digger, preparing a site for the white cross they'd brought. While they struggled to set it upright, Delphie let go of her mother's pant leg and wandered off as if she wanted to put as much distance between herself and Hershall as she could.

Later that day Wren asked Kyle if he'd noticed something in the murky drizzle, a kind of hovering darkness that had followed Hershall as he'd stalked around. At first Wren had thought it was merely the shadow of the husky boy. But mist blanketed the slope and no sun penetrated the heavy cloud cover. She broke into a sweat inside her rain jacket. Whatever was responsible for the ghostly shade trailing the boy definitely wasn't natural.

Kyle *had* noticed the shadow behind Hershall and was profoundly disturbed by it. He'd kept silent about it while they were on the slope hoping to spare Vestie. Kyle didn't doubt that Mencie was also aware and possibly even little Delphie.

The heavy gloom that overlay the slope was not just the normal grayness of a rainy June day. Kyle's whole psyche was edgy and he recognized the symptoms. Whenever he was in the presence of what his Cherokee elders called the Ukdena, the untamed energies of anger and fear that linger just beyond the light of clear thought, Kyle had experienced this same sense of entanglement and impending doom.

The Ukdena were only dangerous when not called into clear light and Kyle doubted that Hershall Lincoln had the inner strength to confront them. The boy could become a positive menace if the Ukdena were to take him over...if they had not already done so.

Because of *his* uncontrolled emotions, Hershall's father, Porter, had become a portal for these spirits of doom and through him, the entire Cove had become vulnerable to discovery and destruction. Was it possible that Hershall was also susceptible to such influences? It seemed all too likely especially if, as Mencie had intimated, Porter's spirit was not yet at rest. Kyle shivered inwardly.

Mencie's inability to locate Porter's body had unsettled Kyle more than he wished to admit. He did not doubt that Porter was dead but he was equally certain that his spirit still roamed. The Ukdena which had enmeshed him were strong here in these Borderlands between the outside world and The Cove. Could Hershall Lincoln, by clutching his hurt and anger so fiercely, also become a doorway for destruction of Cove members? Could Porter's restless spirit find a home in this son who so closely resembled him and who had nearly worshiped him?

Kyle was mulling over these dark suspicions as he worked with Locke to prepare the site for the cross. He also wondered how Wren was dealing with the fact that her mother's body was here, too - buried deeply under this same debris. Wren had chosen not to mention this and he had respected her silence. It seemed too ironic that even in death, Della had not escaped her brother. As Kyle and Locke struggled to erect the cross on a slope that seemed to be rejecting it, Wren eyed Hershall Lincoln's restless prowling uneasily. Only Denver Ray kept forlorn vigil beside their mother.

Zettie, noticing that Delphie had wandered off, went in search of her fey grandchild and discovered her behind a huge boulder, digging in the soft dirt with an excited gleam in her eyes. Zettie touched the child's shoulder and felt a jolt of something akin to recognition. Delphie was connecting to something that Zettie had sought hopelessly for years.

Suddenly Zettie perceived that her daughter Della was somehow near at hand. Hopefully, the old woman knelt beside Delphie and carefully pushed aside a few unusually lovely rocks. Almost at once, she glimpsed something smooth and white in the loose soil. A small moan escaped her trembling lips. Wren, ever alert to where Delphie was, heard Zettie and crossed over the wet slope. Mutely, Delphie pointed to what they had uncovered.

Kneeling beside her Mamaw, Wren delicately touched the bone that Zettie was brushing free of earth. A sweet warmth ran up Wren's arm, a comforting presence that reminded her of the Valley of the Spring. Her mother, Della, had once been a Keeper of the Spring and against all odds, had managed to pass that charge on to her only daughter.

Now Wren, kneeling on the damp earth, closed her eyes and savored a gentle peace emanating from her mother's skeletal remains, bones she had found only to lose again in the rockslide which had claimed Porter's life.

Wren suddenly blinked, her reverie broken by a shy touch on her arm. Delphie pulled a string of dark blue beads from beneath her tee shirt and showed it to Wren with a conspiratorial smile. As Wren cradled the beads in her palm, she experienced a sense of continuity and completion. She finally had something her mother had worn and kept, in both life and death. Her tears mingled with the clean summer rain.

A barely acknowledged anxiety dissipated in Wren's heart – the vexed question of how she would pass on her charge as Keeper of the Spring. The beads promised there would be an answer, in whatever form it would come.

Kyle and Locke finished wedging some stones around the base of the cross and stepped back. It still wasn't perfectly straight but it would have to do. Kyle heard a scuffling sound behind him and noticed that Mencie and the Dean were picking their way across the loose shale toward the large boulder where Delphie and Zettie were kneeling. Wren's yellow rain cap was visible behind them.

Before Kyle could figure out what was going on, Wren, waving eagerly, called him over. He and Locke exchanged glances, shrugged, and started across the slope. Vestie, who had just noticed that Delphie wasn't with her followed quickly.

Wren popped up from behind the boulder, teary-eyed and awe-stricken. "Kyle," she whispered, "I believe Delphie's found Della's bones!"

"No! Can't be!" Kyle mumbled before he looked down into the shallow hole that Zettie and Delphie were scooping out. Suddenly he was on his knees, gently sweeping aside more of the loose dirt. He recognized a couple of the unusual rocks which had once composed the cairn over Della's body.

"Dear God, Wren, I think you may be right," he said softly, carefully removing a few more stones to reveal a human skull.

"I *know* I'm right, Kyle. This is incredible! How could her body be so near the surface now after...after a ton of rock slid down over it?"

"It's the nature of this mountain, honey," Zettie answered as she reached over Wren's shoulder and stroked the skull of her daughter.

"Could be just a bit of her," Locke said dubiously even as his hands twitched to find out. He looked over his shoulder at Mencie who had just taken off her floppy grey hat to beat the water out of it. Without anyone noticing, the rain had stopped and the mist was rolling back to reveal a blue sky.

"Ah'd have a look-see, iffen it were me," she said, a smile as soft as mist passing over her wizened features.

With deft but gentle care, Kyle, Wren, Zettie and Locke began sifting through the damp earth. Delphie was working a couple feet down the slope when Denver Ray leaned over and gave a low whistle. "Holy Cow, she's gone and found some more bones!" Wren scooted toward Delphie who was brushing aside some dirt covering a pile of small bones that were definitely those of a human foot.

Zettie suddenly gave a small cry and snatched up a dirt-stained fragment of cloth. "Hit's her, all right. Ah know this dress. She was wearin' it the last time we saw her...while she was acarryin' you, Winnie chile."

Kyle and Locke continued to carefully turn over the rock-strewn earth while the women brushed the final bits of loam off the bones which were clearly that of a rather small woman. To everyone's surprise, nearly all the bones were in place as if Della had just lain down by this boulder and fallen sleep. Even a bit of reddish hair clung to the back of the skull.

Wren looked up at Mencie who was sitting on the boulder. The gnome-like woman had not taken part in the dis-interring of Della's remains but had remained somewhat aloof, her fey golden eyes watching the process with gentle delight. The Dean purred in her lap, kneading the dusty grey fabric covering her knees.

"What should we do?" Wren asked. Silence fell as they all realized that they had some options regarding Della's remains.

"Mamaw?" Wren reached across the shallow ditch to touch Zettie's arm. "What would you like?"

"Ah, honey," she breathed, "there'd be nothin' Ah'd love more than to see my girl buried in a fittin' way, next to Clyde up in the graveyard behind the church. Could it be done, do you think?" she asked, directing her question to Mencie.

Mencie's eyes gleamed under the shadow of her hat. "Ah don' see why not. She's truly at rest now." She turned toward Wren. "Winnie girl, you remember that night. Seems like she forgave Porter in the end, did she not?"

Wren bowed her head, returning in memory to the storm-tossed clearing about the old Waitsel place. Amid the pain and anger twisting her own heart, Wren could still see the shimmer of Della's presence. She vividly remembered the message Della had asked Wren to convey to Porter on her behalf.

Wren removed her rain hat and brushed her curls back from her face. "Yes, yes, she did," she whispered. Kyle and Locke, who had witnessed that night-time scene, had been unaware of this portion of the drama. But the sweet peacefulness now emanating from Della's remains corroborated Wren's assertion.

Locke's usually grim face softened visibly. "Ah'd like that for her," he said softly. "It don't seem right to leave her out here now that we kin bring her home."

Mencie descended from the rock and flapped her old hat at them. "Do it then!" she commanded and flitted across the littered landscape on some errand of her own.

Locke and Kyle fashioned a traverse from saplings woven together and Wren spread her rain gear over it. Carefully, they collected all the bones they had recovered and lashed them securely onto the impromptu hearse. It proved so light that conveying Della's remains down the steep mountain path was mercifully easy. Everyone but Hershall took turns carrying the litter over the streams that cut across the path and negotiating some of the sharper turns.

Kyle was opposite Wren, each steadying one side of the traverse, when he heard it. Everyone in what had now become a funeral cortege stopped in their tracks. Was it merely the wind swishing through the lush green leaves of early June? Some trick of the air swirling over the boulder strewn slope? It was Vestie who first discerned the melody, the haunting refrain of *"Were you there?"* She began to hum softly and Delphie clutched the tail of her flannel shirt. Denver Ray's head came up and in that moment, the sun glinted off his cobalt blue eyes, so like Vestie's.

"Maw?" he began tentatively.

Vestie lifted her hand to him, a lovely smile breaking across her often bleak features. "They're singin' her home, son," she murmured.

The procession moved forward and soon was met by a group of older men and women coming out from the Cove. Oma and Anson Jack, Jonah, Haidia and Bewley, Tishie, Jerry...the inseparable Garenflo brothers – these and many others were wending their way toward them, singing softly, "Are you here at His risin' from the dead? Oh, are you here at His risin' from the dead? Oh, how it makes us tremble, tremble, tremble ..."

Oma's motherly arm encircled Zettie's small frame in a gesture that said more than words how much she shared her old friend's comfort that she was finally able to give her daughter a seemly resting place. Jonah and Anson Jack went to get a pine coffin from a supply they kept beneath the white church. The community waited prayerfully while Zettie and Winnie, as Wren was known by the Cove community, hurried over to Zettie's cabin for the dress that Zettie had made years earlier for the daughter who had never returned.

Zettie scooped a quilt from her bed and thrust it into Wren's willing arms. Lovingly they arranged the quilt in the pine coffin and stepped back as Locke, who had kept lonely vigil over his sister's remains for over thirty tormented years, placed Della's bones on the soft lining. Tearfully but gratefully, Zettie spread the dress over them and then allowed the men to tap the cover in place.

While this was going on, other men had worked with practiced efficiency, opening a grave beside Clyde Glenning. Wren, standing close to Zettie, heard her whisper tearfully, "She's here, Clyde. Our Della is back with us at last."

Tenderly, Wren wrapped her arm around Zettie's shoulders and drew her close in a reversal of roles, comforting the plucky little lady who was usually the pillar of strength for other aching hearts.

Kyle, stepping back from the grave site, had laid down his shovel and was about to reach for Wren, when he noticed her being surrounded by Cove members. To his chagrin, a stab of jealousy pierced his heart. Even before it fully registered, however, Wren reached out and pulled him to her, laying her head on his broad chest. Gratefully, Kyle brushed the back of his hand over her cheek, damp with tears.

A lean woman with short grey hair stepped toward the head of the grave, the June breeze stirring her cotton dress about her knees. She held a worn copy of The Book in her hands and was leafing through it thoughtfully. Kyle recognized her. It was Tishie, a Faith-Keeper who had prophesied at a momentous Cove gathering some weeks earlier. Silence fell over the group gathered in the cemetery, and Kyle recognized the listening quiet he had begun to associate with group prayer in the Cove.

Tishie's mellow voice mingled with the tranquil twittering of birds in the surrounding woods. "These words from the book of Job express something that's in mah heart jest now as we bring our daughter to lie here among us:

"If you set your heart aright and stretch out your hands toward God, if you remove all iniquity from your conduct, and let not injustice dwell in your tent, surely then you may lift up your face in innocence; you may stand firm and unafraid. For

then you shall forget your misery, or recall it like waters that have ebbed away."

Tishie paused, her head tilted slightly as if listening to an inner echo of these words. Wren swiped at the tears running freely down her cheek and Zettie patted her hand. They could hear the soft rushing of Lovada Branch as it tumbled through The Cove. Tishie raised The Book and continued:

"Then your life shall be brighter than the noonday; its gloom shall become as the morning, and you shall be secure, because there is hope; you shall look round you and lie down in safety, and you shall take your rest with none to disturb. Many shall entreat your favor, but the wicked, looking on, shall be consumed with envy."

Kyle nodded to himself, agreeing that Della had indeed recovered her innocence the moment she had commissioned Wren to forgive Porter. No one now could disturb her rest. Wren squeezed Kyle's arm so tightly that he knew she, too, agreed with Tishie's brief words.

Without further ado, the men moved up to slip some stout ropes under the pine box. Vestie pushed Hershall and Denver Ray forward to assist the men preparing to lower their aunt's body into its final resting place. Both boys seemed a bit spooked but finally Denver Ray lifted the end of one of the ropes. Hershall, however, turned on his heel and strode away, his eyes wild and restless.

Kyle, watching him disappear under the trees, felt certain that the darkness which followed the boy was more than just the natural shade from the leafy canopy. Before Kyle could follow the boy, Locke caught his eye and gestured to him to fill in for Hershall.

Carefully the men let the box down into the deep hole. Before anyone could begin covering the grave, Jonah took The Book from Tishie and flipped back a few pages.

"Jest need to offer these thoughts from Lamentations," he rumbled through his beard. *"Those who were my enemies without cause hunted me down like a bird; they struck me down alive into the pit, and sealed me in with a stone. The waters flowed over my head, and I said, 'I am lost!' I called upon your name, O Lord, from the bottom of the pit; you heard me call...you came to my aid when I called to you; you said, "Have no fear!"*

Zettie raised her head and looked at Jonah gratefully. "My Della is at home now and has naught to fear," she murmured.

Then Zettie held out her hand and Oma placed a wild pink orchid in her palm. Wren recognized it with wonder and surprise for it was the stalk she'd plucked at the Spring a few weeks earlier. How had it stayed so fresh?

Zettie felt Wren's silent question and smiled into her eyes. "Ah jest put the stalk you sent by Mencie into a jug and there it stayed as fresh and purty as the day you picked it fer me. Don' know but it was awaitin' fer my girl, bein' she was a Keeper of the Spring herself. Hit's fittin, don' you know?"

Wren nodded wordlessly and then accepted the bunch of roses and daisies Oma pressed on her. One by one, she passed them out to everyone present who, following Zettie's lead, dropped the blossoms on the pine board lid. Soon it was blanketed with flowers which softened the sounds of clotted earth that the men began to shovel back into the grave. Hershall had not returned but Denver Ray manfully did his share in burying an aunt he had never known, an aunt his father had known far too well.

Before the task was finished, Vestie began to hum and then to sing: "Angel Band." Others joined her, softly offering their prayers of trust and gratitude on behalf of one of their own who indeed, had been taken home by angelic spirits. Little Delphie pressed against her mother's side, uneasy among the crowd of people. Wren, watching Vestie's face, saw her covertly searching the shadows where her older son had disappeared.

Zettie then invited everyone present over to her little house for an impromptu picnic. Women scurried back to their kitchens and soon converged on Zettie's place bringing jars of beets and hard boiled eggs, half a ham, baskets of biscuits and other vittles which they had prepared for their own suppers. A meal of comfort expanded into a feast of gratitude.

If Zettie's heart yearned over the spirit of her son still roaming the borderlands, she did not allow her anxieties to intrude on this moment of celebration for Della's brief life and the unexpected gift of laying her to rest with her kin. Zettie brought out the few photos she had of her daughter and passed them around.

Wren found herself next to Vestie as the two of them studied the face and figure of a woman neither had known but whom both closely resembled. With the addition of fifteen years, Wren was Della in the flesh. Except for her height, Vestie could have been Della's twin. Her hand trembled as she smoothed the photo on her knee while her lips twisted with pain.

"So this here is that Della," she whispered and began to crumple the brittle image. Wren snatched it back and stared hard at Vestie whose cobalt eyes were dark with suppressed rage. Perspiration glimmered on her face as she brushed stray hairs aside with the back of hand. "He...he loved her; never me; always her. He din't like me for nothin' 'cept I had her looks.

"It was her he wanted, always her. He'd call me Della sometimes when we coupled. At first, I thought she was another woman he'd courted when he was away at college. Then, one time when we were back here in The Cove for homecomin', I picked up Zettie's bible and saw her name – Della Lovada – recorded in it. She looked to be born 'bout two years after Locke."

Wren clutched her mother's picture, both horrified and fascinated by Vestie's reaction. Vestie rambled on, lost in her own world. "Ah loved you in the beginnin', Porter. Jest couldn't git over how you'd picked me out – the girl from out back of Turkey Cove. Ah was all alone then, after Granny had passed and ah was so skeered. Seemed like a miracle when an educated man like you took an interest in me. Ah hadn't even got a diploma 'cause Granny took sick my last year of high school and ah stayed home to tend her."

Vestie pulled her heavy braid over shoulder, her graceful fingers plucking it like a dulcimer. "Ah was jest blind, ah guess, believin' you loved me like ah wanted you to. Ah did ever' thin you ever wanted, tryin' and tryin' but seemed like you never quite saw *me,* Vestie! You din't like I was so tall so you'd make me sit in the low rocker on the porch when the evenin' shadders fell. You'd set there then, alookin' at me and sometimes you cried; sometimes you'd git wild and throw me down and take me right there on the floor."

"Thet stopped after the boys got older, a' course. You had *some* feelin' 'bout what was decent, ah guess. But once Delphie was born, all white-gold and with her big dark eyes like my Maw's, you never come near me agin. By then, I'd purt near figured out the story. You was always awantin' Della, hatin' yoreself for it, 'fraid of it....in these last years, you was gittin' positively strange about it.

You started spendin' more time in Lashton of a night and, truth to tell, ah din't keer no more. At least, I'd figured it was Lashton you was goin' to but now ah'm wonderin' iffen' you weren't comin' back here... to her grave. A feller don't git dirt under his fingernails at a whore house. Mebbe you wanted folks to think you was a man almighty with the ladies when, truth was, you was only "hot" after a ghost?"

Wren shuddered as Vestie explored her suspicions aloud. It fit what she had seen of Porter that last time...the night he'd mistaken her for her mother. The horror of those stormy hours still haunted Wren's dreams. Should she tell Vestie the whole story or leave it as Locke had described the event? If she did tell Vestie, there was only one place where she could risk it – one place where Porter's restless spirit couldn't reach them.

Just as Wren was pondering her options, Hershall Lincoln slithered out of the dark woods not ten feet from where she and Vestie were sitting. He said nothing as he passed them but Wren shivered as if Hershall was trailed by a chill shade.

Vestie rocked slightly, hugging herself, "Hit kin kill a woman to know she's jest a stand-in fer someone else, you know?" Wren studied Vestie, profiled against a field winking with fireflies. Porter had nearly slain the spirit of this lovely woman as truly as he had destroyed Wren's mother. They had just buried Della. Clenching her fists, Wren determined that Vestie would get the chance for life Della never had.

Cautiously, Wren stroked Vestie's slumped shoulders. "I'm so sorry, Vestie, so very sorry. I... I'd... there's some things I want you to know...to tell you... not now but before we go back..."

To Wren's disappointment, the mountain woman failed to respond to her tentative overture. Instead she shrugged off Wren's hand and got up muttering about having to find Delphie.

Hurt and mystified, Wren watched Vestie's figure merge into the crowd of women packing up their baskets and totes. For a brief moment, Vestie had revealed something of herself to Wren and then she had disappeared - much like Delphie melting back into the forest. How could she gain Vestie's trust, help her recover her spirit, her life?

Thoughtfully, Wren wound her way among the people in Zettie's yard until she reached the chair where her little Mamaw rested, with her hand smoothing Delphie's light hair.

"Mamaw?" Wren began hesitantly, "Mamaw, how can I...do you think...would you know...?"

Zettie smiled gently, "You worried about Vestie, Winnie Lovada?"

Wren nodded but before she could say more, Vestie strode over, took Delphie's hand and pulled her away. In the deepening twilight Vestie's features were as blank as mannequin's, her eyes dark and expressionless.

Zettie silently watched her go and then turned back to Wren. "Sit you here by me, Winnie girl, and listen up. You're given a burden you din't ast for. As Porter's daughter, you're called on to look after the hurts he left behind. Vestie is your "bundle," honey, even if she's strange with you. I hope you'll be willin' to help her ifn' she'll let you."

Wren looked down at her clasped hands and sighed. "I'm willing, Mamaw, but... sometimes she seems to let me in, other times it's like she slams the door in my face. Maybe this sounds selfish but I believe if I can do something for her, I'll be helping myself as well. There's three of us, Vestie, Della, and myself, who have been wounded by Porter...and maybe we can only find healing together?"

Wren looked up into Zettie's pain-filled eyes and suddenly realized she needed to add Zettie to the list as well. And Delphie? Yes, she, too. The child had been rejected by Porter since her birth. That made five lives, inseparably linked, stretching across three generations, which were injured, only one (so far) mortally, by Porter's treachery. With a sudden awakening, Wren realized she was uniquely placed to mediate their healing ...that this was part of what being a Keeper of the Spring meant.

Wren felt Zettie's steady gaze and knew that the older woman was privy to her unspoken train of thought. Zettie patted Wren's hand and nodded approvingly, before she observed softly, "Ah hated to see what was happenin' to Vestie over the years and ah so wanted to help her. But somehow she knew I couldn't, or wouldn't, lay any blame on my son and so she never let me get close to her. Ah wasn't a Keeper anymore – that had already passed on to Della and through her, to you...but yore time had'na come yet..."

Zettie's gentle touch changed to a painful crunching of Wren's fingers. "Hit's yore charge now, gal, and the lives of five Lovada women depend on how you fulfill it. And more than jest us need you, Winnie. I suspect you are one of the few means of redemption left to Porter. He needs you, too. And," Zettie paused and took a deep breath, "Ah suspect his boys do, too, 'specially Hershall Lincoln."

Wren stiffened, "Wasn't it enough that I forgave Porter? And that I offered him Della's forgiveness?"

Zettie stroked Wren's fingers. "Ah know, tain't fair to ask you to try to undo all the harm he did ...but life ain't about fairness, honey, surely you know that by now. And it's not simply 'bout justice neither. There's somethin' larger, bigger even than that. We all need it – need to get it; need to give it. And the only word I know for it is mercy."

Wren felt tears fill her eyes as Zettie's gentle words echoed in her own heart. What she and Kyle had found at the Spring was mercy ...and it had saved them; given their marriage a new beginning; and given them both a mission in life.

Zettie's soft voice continued, "Winnie Lovada, you are the Keeper of the Spring now and it is not only your right but your duty to take anyone back there who needs it. Most all the folks in The Cove have been there at least onct. I took many there in my time. Your Maw, Della, didn't get the chanct to do thet so hit's bin over thirty year since anyone's bin there 'ceptin' jest you'ns last month." Zettie's glance took in Kyle who had silently joined Wren and was now squatting beside her.

Wren reached for Kyle's hand. "Kyle hon, Mamaw and I – we're talking about Vestie. I know you're concerned about her, too. I'm wondering if I should take her to The Spring."

Kyle rubbed his nose, a thoughtful expression on his face. Finally a wry smile touched his lips. "Well, if you can get her to go with you, she'll not come back the same person as she goes in!"

Wren nodded in agreement, rubbing her hands ruefully through her tangled hair. "True enough, Kyle, all too true!"

Wren caught sight of Vestie handing some bedrolls to her boys as they prepared to go to Oma's for the night. Delphie stood apart from the little group, her large eyes gleaming like that of a cat in the night. Wren felt a surge of fear for the child. But from what? She noticed that Zettie was also studying the family and wondered if she, too, felt uneasy about Delphie. With her focus on Vestie though, Wren decided it was not yet time to tend this growing concern about Delphie.

As the June evening deepened, the Cove folks had gathered up their empty baskets and totes, leaving a generous supply of left-overs so Zettie could more easily feed her visiting family. Neither the Glennings nor Wren and Kyle were in any hurry to leave The Cove. The healing peace that filled the broad valley through which Lovada Branch flowed was balm to their bruised spirits. Even Hershall seemed to have calmed down as the evening wore on.

Wren doubted that Vestie would insist she had to go back to Panther Gap right away if Wren offered to take her back to the Spring. Zettie gave Wren a little push and nodded toward Vestie. "Best ketch her afore she sets out for Oma's place," she whispered.

Agreeing, Wren got up quickly and hurried toward Vestie, rehearsing words that might penetrate Vestie's self-protective indifference. She reached the Glenning family just as they were starting down the road toward Oma's large house where visitors to the Cove were usually put-up. Quick-eared Delphie turned at Wren's approach, smiled and reached for her hand. The trusting gesture warmed Wren's heart and encouraged her.

"Vestie?" Wren asked softly. "Vestie, can I ask you something?"

Wordlessly, Vestie gestured to her boys to go on ahead of them and then turned toward Wren. It was too dark for Wren to read Vestie's face so she had to risk speaking without any hint of how her words would be received. "I was listening to all you were saying back there, Vestie, and…and it struck me that it might be good for you – if you wanted - to go back to The Spring with me."

Vestie's head went up and she stroked the heavy braid that lay over her breast. "To The Spring? Why would you offer me thet? Ah'm not…not worthy to go there. Thet's jest fer those who belong, inn't?"

"Vestie, it's for all of us…all of us that need its gifts," adding softly, "for all of us that need grace."

In the dim glow from the rising moon, Wren saw a glimmer of tears on Vestie's cheeks. "Even fer me?" she whispered.

"Especially you," Wren answered firmly. "I'll come for you in the morning." Before Vestie could refuse, Wren turned and hurried back to Zettie and Kyle. "It's done. We'll go in the morning," she said, unaware of a new note of assurance in her voice and manner. Kyle glanced over at Zettie and caught a gleam of satisfaction in her eye as she lifted a lantern and led them into her house for the night. Wren had donned the mantle of The Keeper.

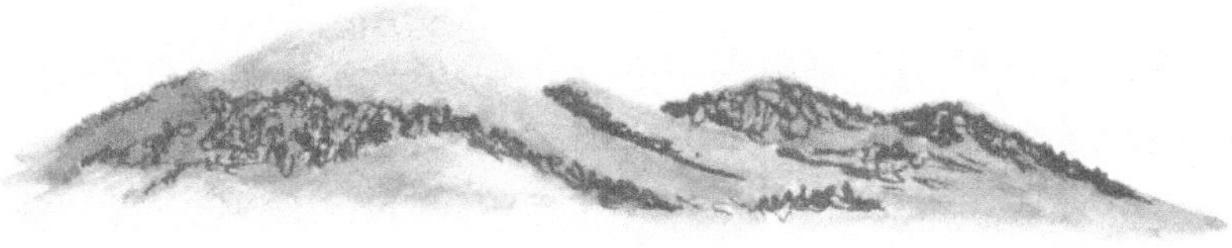

CHAPTER SEVEN

The morning rose rain-washed and clear as Wren stepped off Zettie's porch. Myriad scents greeted her. The orange blossom leaning by the steps, the dampness of earth, the sweetness of cut grass – each offered a distinct delight that mingled with Wren's concerns about Vestie and transformed them into quiet confidence as she walked up the road to Oma and Jack's big farmhouse.

Wren found Vestie sitting on the long porch that ran along two sides of the house. Her eyes were closed, her head resting on the high back of a wicker rocker.

Her hands were still for once, allowing Wren to observe not only their natural grace but also how work-worn and aged beyond their time they were. These were the fingers that danced over the dulcimer but which had also grubbed tobacco, peeled vegetables and scrubbed tubs of blue jeans in what Wren suspected was a thankless round.

Fine lines already creased Vestie's sun-browned face and in repose, she looked profoundly sad. Her natural beauty was fading, hastened by Porter's treatment and now, that of her sons. Wren's resolve hardened. She *would* help Vestie recover herself…her gifts and her dignity. At the sound of Wren's boot on the gravel, Vestie stirred and her face brightened.

"He said you wouldn't come," she commented softly, "and I was just as glad. No call for you to waste your time with me."

Wren puckered her brow. "Who said I wouldn't come?"

"Hershall," Vestie responded. "Said I wasn't your kind, bein' jest a farm gal and all."

Wren kicked the step of the porch sharply, "Vestie! Why do you listen to him? He's only a kid, flapping his lip. Where is he?"

"Jonah come over fer 'im first thing this mornin'," Vestie revealed. "Hershall, he din't want to go with Jonah but I reckon in the end he din't have no choice."

Wren dipped her head to hide a quick grin. If Jonah had taken Hershall in hand, she almost felt pity for the lad. Kyle had once experienced some of Jonah's "mentoring" and later confessed to Wren that the older man pulled no punches.

"Just what Hershall needs," Wren declared. "Neither Kyle nor Locke seem to have much influence over that boy." Vestie allowed herself a nod of agreement.

Vestie had already seen that her boy's anger was breaking out in uncontrollable bursts of rage. There was no denying that dark influences were shadowing him. At the very least, Jonah would keep Hershall from trying to follow the two women to the Spring, something Kyle had warned Wren he might try.

"Where's Denver Ray?" Wren asked, knowing that the two boys were usually inseparable.

Vestie's smile deepened. "Jerry Hatcher's offered to teach him how to track."

"Not us, I trust," Wren commented. Jerry Hatcher was a full-blooded Cherokee and one of the Guardians of the Cove. He had risen to speak at a Meeting Wren and Kyle had attended some weeks earlier when Cove members were seeking a means to protect the community from discovery. His visionary contribution had convinced Wren of his deep connection with the spirits of Unaka Mountain on whose broad flank The Cove was situated.

Since Jerry had offered to teach Denver Ray Native American skills and Jonah had taken Hershall in hand, Wren suspected a kindly conspiracy was afoot. Obviously the elders of The Cove were at work trying to defuse the threat that Porter's restless spirit posed for his vulnerable sons.

"Delphie?" Wren inquired. Vestie lifted her chin, pointing toward the side of the house where Oma sat with Delphie at her feet, the child absorbed in learning how to weave on a lap frame. Wren quickly divined that Vestie wasn't too happy that her own little shadow had shifted her trust to someone besides herself so she made no comment. Instead she just said that Zettie had packed a lunch for both of them, indicating the small backpack slung over her shoulder.

Vestie rose slowly, almost reluctantly. If her hesitance was due to fear, Wren had no reassurance to offer for Vestie had reason to be afraid. No one went to the Spring and returned unchanged. Silently, the two women set out following the rippling stream of Lovada Branch up the eastern slope of The Cove.

Wren had only made the trip to the Spring once before and that time, she had been aided by the silver medallion that had been her keepsake since birth. She had left the medal at The Spring, in the cave behind the falls, as her sacrificial gift which joined a dozen or more similar pendants left there by earlier Keepers of the Spring. Wren was uncertain if she could find the Spring without it but felt that, for Vestie's sake, she had to try.

By mid-morning, Lovada Branch had shrunk to a narrow and very shallow trickle of water which suddenly disappeared altogether beneath a huge boulder. Wren felt panic rising ...she knew they weren't yet at the Spring, the source of Lovada Branch, but a strange blankness blurred her memory of her earlier trek. How she wished for some of Kyle's woods' lore though it hadn't assisted *him* on their first (and only) pilgrimage to The Spring. Wren leaned against the boulder, trying to calm herself, seeking strength from the ancient rock itself. Vestie stood back, arms crossed over her chest, her cobalt-blue eyes hooded and distant. Did she doubt Wren's ability to find The Spring? Or her own readiness to face what she might find there?

Wren ran her hand over the sun-warmed surface of the rock and suddenly, the rough stone seemed to quiver. She stopped and waited. Yes! She could detect a slight ripple in the rock where she was leaning and shifted her position experimentally. The sensation grew stronger. Cautiously Wren slid further around the stone and experienced a tingling in her feet that ran up her calves. Without thinking she unlaced her boots and peeled off her socks. Now she remembered. All she had to do was follow an underground stream that she could detect through the soles of her feet!

Vestie watched Wren, lifting her eyebrows in an unspoken question. Wren nodded and set out across a grassy bald, a natural meadow in the high mountains where no trees had taken root. Step by step, Wren proceeded gradually downhill toward a rocky gorge with Vestie following, curious but silent. Once within the cool shadows of the narrowing glen, both women heard the roar of a high cascade.

"We're coming closer," Wren whispered as they approached an ancient hemlock sprouting from a rock that blocked the trail they were on.

Wren halted and pushed Vestie ahead of her. "Go!" she hissed, some instinct instructing her that at this point, Vestie had to find the way herself, proving she was accepted by the Spring. Vestie stopped, perplexed, while her eyes darted about the towering cliffs that boxed them in. Then she studied the twisted hemlock with its soft, trailing branches. Wren smiled in relief when Vestie dropped to her knees and began to crawl under the low boughs. Just as she disappeared from sight, Wren stooped and followed Vestie through a narrow cleft in the rock wholly concealed by the ancient tree.

When Wren slipped out of the shadowed niche, she spotted Vestie standing in liquid sun light, her head cocked with delight as myriads of birds serenaded her. They flitted in and out of the foliage where they nested like shimmering jewels. Lovada Branch itself re-surfaced not far from them, gurgling and chuckling merrily as it flowed over its rocky bed. Vestie turned toward Wren, a silent "oh" of astonishment shaping her lips.

"May I?" she murmured.

Wren smiled gently and nodded, "They await you."

The look of alarm that crossed Vestie's face reminded Wren of her own first reaction to the Spring. Before she could reassure Vestie, a gentle chuckling filled the air, a swell of merriment that was totally disarming. Vestie's incipient panic melted away and she took a few tentative steps deeper into the valley, scanning the fresh loveliness that surrounded them. Louder than all else, the roar of falling water drew the two women inexorably forward.

Rounding a stand of Great Laurel that towered over them, Wren and Vestie suddenly shielded their eyes from a silvery glare bouncing off a wall of water directly in front of them. Wren watched Vestie raise her eyes to the geyser that leapt from the brink thirty feet above their heads. The late morning sun playing through the misting spray created rainbows that shimmered, arched and disappeared into the swirling basin by their feet.

A breeze stroked Vestie's sweaty hair back from her forehead as tenderly as a mother welcoming home a long-awaited daughter. Vestie stumbled backward, moaning something unintelligible to Wren. Then, before Wren could stop her, she swirled around and disappeared behind the glistening laurel. Wren smiled. Had not she and Kyle done the same thing the first time they'd seen the Spring?

Quietly Wren sank to the damp grass at the pool's edge, content to let Vestie absorb the experience of the valley in whatever way the spirits led her. Vestie was now in the charge of Others and Wren knew better than to interfere. She could neither shield nor guide Vestie at this point. She could only pray that this lovely, wounded woman would accept the truths she must face and find healing in that acceptance.

Drawing up her knees, Wren rested her chin on them, allowing herself to be mesmerized by the dancing waters before her. Memories of her earlier experience at the Spring returned, vivified by recent events. A deeper understanding of the task laid upon her overwhelmed Wren and she lost all track of time. The sun was burning her shoulders through her tee shirt when she suddenly returned to herself. Where was Vestie?

Wren jumped up, brushing damp grit from the seat of her jeans, and retraced her steps around the Great Laurel. No Vestie. Wren wanted to call out but something prevented her. The music of the valley was too lovely to be disturbed by her anxious cries. Instead, Wren followed the verge of Lovada Branch as it meandered back through the lush valley. A flash of blue caught Wren's eye as an indigo bunting swept past her. Following its flight, Wren saw Vestie sitting with her back against the bark of a great tulip poplar. A dappled fawn rested its delicate head in her lap

Silently Wren crossed the grassy expanse that separated them but she stopped abruptly when an invisible hand restrained her. Though Wren could see Vestie clearly, she doubted that Vestie knew she was there. Vestie was crooning softly to the little creature she was stroking. The fawn's mother grazed off to one side, unconcerned that her baby was inching its way into Vestie's lap.

Wren watched various emotions chase themselves across Vestie's tanned features. Her braid had come undone and her auburn hair rippled over her shoulders. Suddenly Wren noticed that Vestie was stark naked. Her wet clothes lay in a heap beside her. What had happened? The doe glanced up when she caught Wren's scent on the breeze and gave a snort of warning. Her fawn responded, struggling to unfold its spindly legs. Gently Vestie supported the gangly creature until it was steady on its tiny hooves and able to dance over to its watchful mother.

"I'm sorry," Wren whispered softly, "I didn't mean to scare it."

Vestie smiled and shook her head. "'Twasn't meant to last. It don't need to, I guess. Not likely I'll ever fergit *that*." She glanced down where the fawn had lain and her nakedness suddenly seemed to register. "Oh, my land, what must you think?" she gasped, her hand to her mouth as she reached out for her soggy clothes.

"I didn't think anything of it, Vestie," Wren assured her. "Here," she spread her arms in a wide arc encompassing the valley, "neither shame nor blame have place. Let me spread out your stuff in the sun so it will dry faster."

Shaking out Vestie's jeans, Wren ventured, "What happened, if I may ask?"

The familiar shuttered look crossed Vestie's face but then she threw back her head, shook out her hair and a smile lit up her cobalt eyes. Gazing through her thick lashes, she mulled, "I don't rightly know how to tell it, Wren. Ever since I came into this place, it was like I heerd voices all 'round me. Kindly voices – like my Grannie's. It skeered me some 'specially when I began to listen to what They was sayin'. They started me recollectin' my life ...and all what's happened."

"All that's happened?" Wren prompted.

"You shore you want to know?" Vestie asked shyly.

"If you want to tell me, yes, I'd like to know." Wren lowered herself to the grass next to Vestie, staring with her at the sparkling water of the young Lovada Branch.

Vestie began softly, "Ah don't 'member much 'bout my Maw 'ceptin' she liked to sing. She and me lived with Granny since I was a young 'un. I 'spect she hadn't never married my Pa, whoever he was. She went off to work in Asheville after a time and would send money back to us – we sorely needed it. It weren't all that much even so, but little by little, it stopped comin'. One day I came in from school and Granny was asettin' by the farr jest not doin' nothin'. I knew right off somethin' bad had happened.

"Maw's dead, ain't she?" I ast and Granny jest picked me up and set me on her lap. She tole me that the police had stopped by that afternoon and said there'd been a fight at the place where Maw was singin'. Some one had a gun and... no one knew for sure how it all went but Maw got shot and died right off."

"Vestie!" Wren breathed, touching the sun-browned arm as Vestie told her story in a voice so dreamy and detached that it might have been about someone else. "How awful for you!"

"Ah guess," Vestie shrugged. "After that, it was really tough. Granny had a small 'bacca allotment and between the two of us, we'd set the plants and weed'em and top'em and chop'em and stake'em and hang'em fer dryin'. It was turrible hard work fer an old woman and a girl but it was the onliest way we could git cash money. Granny made me go to school as much as she could but there was times when she needed me on account of all the work.

Still don't know how she did it all. Kilt her in the end, ah figured. She jest lay down one day and din't git up. It was my last year to school. I stayed home and looked after her. The neighbors were real good to help me out all through that year. The Doctor he said there was nothin' he could do. Her heart was jest plumb wore out."

Vestie paused and plucked a stalk of tiny blue speedwell from the grass. “I’ve not thought about Granny fer years. This place seems to bring her back…makes me remember what I was afore I married Porter. After Granny died, I sold the homeplace fer what I could git, took my clothes and dulcimer and went to Lashton. I’d read about a college there that was payin’ folks to sing the old ballads and thought mebbe I could sing fer them. Turns out, I could. They was all excited ‘bout some of the old love songs Granny had taught me. Hadn’t even heard some of them the way I’d learnt them from her. I was so proud to be able to make my own way doin’ what Granny had taught me.”

Vestie’s face was glowing and the beauty which years of drudgery had drained off reappeared as if a veil had been whisked away. Wren watched with delight. “That must have been so grand for you, Vestie! I’m sure your Granny would have been proud of you.”

Vestie’s radiance dimmed, “That’s where I met Porter – at one of the programs where I was singin’. He jest seemed to fall fer me…but it weren’t really me he saw or wanted. I only figured that out later – too much later.”

Vestie sighed, “What did I know then – I was so young and lonely. He courted me some six weeks a’fore he convinced me to marry him. I planned to keep on singing but no, it was almost as if he were shamed to have me seen. He wouldn’t let me leave the farm fer nothin’. The boys was born and I loved ’em …but he turned’ em agin’ me somehow. The onliest thang he din’t take from me was Delphie. Somehow, he was afraid of her but she don’t know that… nor does she now. She never could trust him – allas runnin’ off into the woods whenever he was around. And she never, ever said anythin’, not nary a word. She’s not deaf, that much I know. Wouldn’t s’prize me if’n she heerd the grass a’ growin’. I know fer a fact that she talks with the wild things…but not to folks.” Vestie paused before she went on bitterly.

"She ain't slow like *he* said...but he'd never even let me take her to see a specialist to see what was wrong. Seems like he'd druther she *didn't* talk none." Vestie lifted her shoulders and spread her hands helplessly. "Why din't I figure that out 'till now? I was jest gettin' so beat down by then, I 'most forgot how to talk even to myself. I didn't even dare to sing when he was around. He threatened to smash Granny's dulcimer 'till I jest took to hidin' it when he was in the house. Towards the end there, he jest used me. It was like he owned me, body and soul. He kept tryin' to make me into *her.*"

"Her?" Wren asked though she knew.

"Della," Vestie said softly, "Yore Maw. Until I met you last month with Locke, I din't know for sure what he'd done to her. No one ever talked about her. Like I said, it was only after I sneaked a peak in Mamaw's Bible, that I knew who this "Della" was."

Wren looked at Vestie squarely. "Well, you know now – and you know what I am."

"That don't matter to me, honey," Vestie said gently. "You are who you make yourself, not what others make you. Wisht I'd always felt thet way. But now, now I know that I am ...well, I'm okay, too – even me, pore Vestie!"

Wren saw a thin, sad smile touch Vestie's lips before she continued, "Thet's what these here Voices bin tellin' me today." Vestie looked down in wonder at her glistening body. "There's a pool over yonder and thet's where it happened. It's a right strong whirlpool and I figured I could get sucked under and jest drown..."

Wren looked up, startled. "You wanted to drown yourself? Here? Why? What made you feel that bad, that terrible?"

Vestie glanced anxiously toward Wren, trying to gauge her reaction, seeking some understanding. "This place here, it seems jest too...well, mebbe the word is *pure*? And then there is the Voices...they keep telling me stuff ah cain't hardly believe. Like ah'm strong, good...when ah know ah'm jest hollow inside, so empty there's nothin' to me...it got so's I jest couldn't stand all the argufyin' in my head..."

Wren gently touched Vestie's shoulder, trying to convey that she knew exactly what Vestie had felt...that she, too, had once decided the world would be better off shed of her and what she was.

Vestie's mouth curved in rueful response. "But you can't drown here, kin you? I throwed myself into that foaming water and it was like...like a hunderd lovin' hands jest kotched me up, whirled me around over and over but oh, so gentle-like... I felt like a babe, washed and clean and rocked back and forth. I jest knew I could relax and...and, oh, trust Them?" Once again Vestie looked uncertainly at Wren.

"You can trust Them," Wren affirmed.

"Then, They dunked me!" Vestie's light laugh rang out and wakened echoes.

"Dunked you?" Wren asked, even as she recalled Kyle's account of his experience in Lovada Branch. "Did you feel betrayed?"

Vestie pursed her lips thoughtfully, "No, strange to tell it, I didn't. It was as if I knew They was playing with me...like I was invited to be a little 'un and then grow up all over agin. Only this time, I growed up loved by...by," she groped and tears sparkled on her cheeks. "loved by One who would never leave me, never hurt me, *always* be there... here...wherever." The brilliant smile that lit up Vestie's face at that moment took Wren's breath away. She watched Vestie rise gracefully and walk into the full sun, the wind rippling her hair about her slender body, and begin to sing the old Gospel song, "Shall We Gather at the River?"

Wren told Kyle later that she would never forget the sheer loveliness of Vestie's rich voice swelling and filling the glen, and echoing back from the rocky walls surrounding them, like an ethereal descant. Did a bright cloud enfold them? Or did

Wren's eyes simply mist at the sheer beauty of the moment? Perhaps even the birds stopped and listened. Wren recalled seeing the doe and her fawn standing on either side of Vestie, lit up by the same light that surrounded her. Wren had wished the vision would never end.

Overcome, she closed her eyes and when she opened them, only Vestie was there, calmly donning her now dry jeans and shirt. All that remained of the radiance they had just shared was a flame kindled deep in Vestie's blue eyes and a shining moment enshrined in Wren's heart.

Slowly Wren spread the lunch that Zettie had packed for them and to their surprise, both women realized they were ravenously hungry. "Good thing Mamaw Zettie sent enough for a small army," Vestie giggled as she licked the chocolate frosting from her fingers after her third brownie.

Wren nodded appreciatively as she downed more of the sweet tea from a tall thermos. "If Kyle were here, he'd be joking about another miracle of the loaves and fishes."

At the reference to Kyle, Vestie flicked a speculative glance toward Wren and Wren felt the question trembling behind her eyes. By now, the comfort she felt with Vestie was such that she knew there could be no secrets between them. It was time...

"Yes, Vestie, Kyle's a priest," Wren responded to her unvoiced question. "He was ordained up north."

"But he's not workin' as a preacher now. Did...did somethin' happen?" Vestie suddenly covered her mouth. "Now mebbe I shouldn't be astin' you thet. It's not none of my business, no how."

"Don't worry about that, Vestie, I do want to tell you more about Kyle and me, but there's something else I need to tell you while we're still here," Wren said, waving her hand around the valley.

Vestie looked up from the backpack she was filling with leftovers. "Hit's about Porter?"

"Yes. Locke didn't tell you all that happened the night he died," Wren began, "He didn't want to, not with your boys standing there."

Vestie sighed. "I figured as much. Later, when I went over the story he'd told us that day, I felt there was somethin' strange about it. First off, it didn't make much sense that the four of you was out on the mountain at night with a storm comin' on."

"The Elders sent me out; sent Kyle, too," Wren began, her voice thin and strained as she revisited the harrowing events of that night. "No one knew for sure if Porter was out there, though some had their suspicions. Mencie's usually aware whenever someone is crossing through the Borderlands. Locke had been trying to track Porter down but he'd lost the trail. That wouldn't have happened unless Porter deliberately threw him off."

Vestie frowned as Wren told her of the long years that Locke had kept watch on his brother. Lately he'd realized that Porter's mind was being slowly eroded by the weight of guilt and self-deception he carried. Wren's throat tightened up as she added, "Locke knew that it was Porter who had raped Della; and that was why she was so horrified by her pregnancy."

"How'd he learn it?" Vestie whispered, as she sat hugging her knees.

"Mencie found Della on the trail as she was coming back from the Spring. Della had gone there after I was born. It was something she needed to do but she went too soon. She was hemorrhaging badly by the time Mencie reached her. Della told Mencie everything, including where she'd left me. She gave her the medallion that was to be mine as a Keeper of the Spring. It usually passes from mother to daughter," Wren explained.

Vestie merely nodded.

"Then Mencie gave the medal to Locke and told him where to find me. He did that but never told my foster Mom who he was ... or who I was either. He was afraid that if I knew too soon, I'd try to find my true family...which would have revealed what Porter had done. And...and he suspected that Porter would kill me to prevent the truth from coming out."

Vestie pressed her knuckles against her lips and whispered, "Ah think Locke was right to fear thet. Lord, thet man had a mean streak a mile wide."

Wren's compassion welled up, conscious that Vestie had experienced that meanness first hand for almost twenty years. "Did Porter get worse toward the end?"

"Yeh," Vestie breathed softly, "yeh, he was near out of his head at times. Folks who knowed him at the school would've never recognized him when the broodin' overtook him. Haunted, he was, like he was seein' things no one else did. Ah tried to keep the kids away from him then. The boys, they didn't understand... ah reckon they figured I was the strange one... and mebbe I am. He'd made them think I couldn't do nothin'. Made me believe it, too. Don't know how he done it..." Vestie's voice trailed off.

Wren waited. When Vestie said nothing further, she ask softly, "Do you still believe it, Vestie?"

Vestie ran her fingers through her long hair and began to braid it as she pondered Wren's question. By the time she slipped a band over the neat braid, Vestie was smiling. She tossed it over her shoulder, "Not no more, I don't," she declared. "Ah feel like ah've bin set free, set free from somethin' dark and evil. Ah've got a chancet at life now." Vestie licked her lips, "Ah hope thet don't sound so selfish... to be glad my man is dead so ah kin finally begin to live...?"

Wren put her arm around Vestie's shoulders. "You're not the first woman to feel that way, Vestie. And it is not your fault that things got so bad," Wren added firmly, "Towards the end, Vestie, I think Porter was so torn up inside with guilt and fear and shame, he didn't know what he wanted. He was a haunted man, just like you said."

"Aw right, now tell me," Vestie demanded, issuing the invitation Wren had been waiting for. "Tell me everything that happened that last night."

Wren took a deep breath. "You know those times when he didn't come home, Vestie? When he let the guys think he was hanging out in Lashton? The truth was he was coming back here to The Cove to visit Della's grave. He kept adding stones and rocks to the little cairn Mencie had laid out to mark the site. Locke told me he'd seen Porter lugging boulders so heavy it was near impossible to carry them. Most of them were beautiful – Locke didn't know if he was trying to atone for what had happened by beautifying Della's grave ...or he feared someone would find her body and he was trying to bury her even deeper. Either way, he seemed to be punishing himself."

Vestie's lips twitched but she didn't say anything.

"On the night he died, Porter took me there..."

"To her grave?" Vestie asked, horror and pity in her voice.

"Yes. He practically dragged me through the woods. It was dark and the wind was rising but he knew the way even without a light. He started talking to himself and then I really got scared. When the lightning flashed, I could see he was sweating. Spittle was running out of his mouth... and his eyes... they were wild. When we got to the clearing at the old Waitsel place, I truly didn't know what was going on in his mind but..." Wren licked her dry lips, "I... I felt like he wanted to kill me, kill me there, at Della's grave!

"I tripped over one of the loose rocks lying around and he grabbed the front of my shirt ..." Wren shuddered and reached out for Vestie's hand. "He started shaking me and hollering the most awful stuff. Then he pushed me down on the ground like he was going to pound my head on the rocks or...or...." Vestie's warm hand squeezed Wren's fingers and she nodded so knowingly that Wren felt she understood as no one else could have.

Wren continued grimly, "I somehow wriggled out from under him and got up on my feet. I started to back off and by then, Locke and Kyle were there. Locke caught me just as I tripped again and then Kyle had me in his arms..." Wren drew in a shuddering breath. "God, Vestie, just telling it, even here, shakes me up. I don't know what Locke told Porter but suddenly he turned as limp as an old rag. I think by then all he wanted was out of his misery ... he even begged me to *kill* him!"

"Did you?" Vestie asked with deadly calm.

Wren sighed, looking inward, even as she shook her head. "I couldn't. Seeing him there, so hideous and at the same time, so pitiful, all the anger and bitterness in me just dissolved. I had Kyle's hunting knife in my hand and I don't think either of the guys would have stopped me. But..." Wren shrugged, "I don't know, he didn't seem worth it.

"And, Vestie, this is the strangest part of all, it was like the woods and wind and even the rocks, were moaning that old song, 'Oh, Death.' And I could see the terror in Porter's eyes. I just knew that if I killed him, the mountain would have to drink his blood, the wind would have to carry his last cry, and nothing, nothing, could ever bury what I did deep enough. The darkness I'd unleashed would destroy not just me but everything The Cove stood for."

Vestie stared hard at Wren. "Well, what *did* happen then? Youn's lived. You came back. But he is dead."

"Yes, he's dead ...mostly," Wren whispered. "I wish I could feel we are done with him, that what he started has ended there under the rock slide. The mountain tried but it can only do so much." Wren look sadly at Vestie. "Watch the boys and, Vestie, especially protect Delphie. It's not over yet." Vestie said nothing but Wren read both fear and anger on her face and ached for her.

"Truthfully, none of us can figure out what really happened that night," Wren admitted, picking up her narrative. "I doubt we ever will. Lightning and thunder was rocking the ground. Then Porter told us it was the dynamite charges that were set up on a sequence by the forest service. Suddenly he started grinning, like he was going to get everything he wanted after all. He had realized that the lightning had tripped off the charges and knew that at least one charge was buried right there in the clearing."

"I think Kyle figured out what might happen because he grabbed me then. We started to run with Locke right behind us. Then I realized Porter wasn't with us. He had just laid himself down on the rocks of the cairn, as peaceful as I'd ever seen him. Somehow I just couldn't leave him there. The guys tried to stop me but I ran back and started to tug at him. He *was* my father, after all.

"Locke and Kyle came up and took hold, too and we managed to drag him out of the clearing. We'd only gone a short way when he broke loose from Locke and Kyle, grabbed me and threw me down into a gully. Kyle jumped in after me. Then, I don't know, Locke and Porter were fighting...but I really couldn't see anything. Later Locke told me that Porter tripped him and then started running back toward the clearing...

"Where Della's grave was," Vestie said softly.

"Yes! He was calling her name when there was another explosion right above the Waitsel place which set off a big rockslide. Locke rolled down into the gully on top of us just as rocks and dirt and trees blew overhead. Being down in the wash saved our lives. But pretty soon, we could hear a flood roaring down the creek bed. We scrambled out just in time.

"Once it started to grow lighter, all we could see was mud and toppled trees and rocks... boulders. It was like the bones of the mountain were laid bare. But we didn't see anything of Porter."

Vestie wrapped her arms around Wren. "You did all you could, honey. More than most would have." Vestie looked thoughtfully toward the shimmering surface of Lovada Branch. "What do you think? Was he trying to kill you or save you?"

"I've wondered a lot about that," Wren said, shaking her head slowly, "but I haven't found any answer. Porter knew where the dynamite charges were laid because he was the one who'd made the deal with the Forest Service and shown the Cherokee scouts where to mark the trail for the road into the Cove."

"You mean, he was meanin' to betray Lovada Cove?" Vestie asked in shock.

"It looks like that," Wren said sadly. "When Porter ran back toward the clearing, I thought maybe he wanted to save Della's body or…" Wren shrugged and whispered, "all I know is what I *hope…* that in the end he wanted to save us and he didn't care what happened to himself."

"Oh God," Vestie moaned and wrapped her arms around herself. "No one deserves to die like thet but ah bet, ah jest bet, he wanted to die and the mountain claimed him."

"It seems so," Wren agreed, relieved that Vestie had been ready for this much of the story. There was more but Wren felt it could wait. Vestie needed to look forward now. Porter was the past. Healing would take a long time but at least, it was beginning.

The music of falling waters filled the secret gorge, soothing both women and offering them a new kind of peace. They pulled on their boots and prepared to hike back to The Cove on a path that would be wiped from Vestie's memory as soon as she left. What had happened in the Valley of the Spring, however, was etched indelibly on her soul and would forever alter how she viewed both herself and her past.

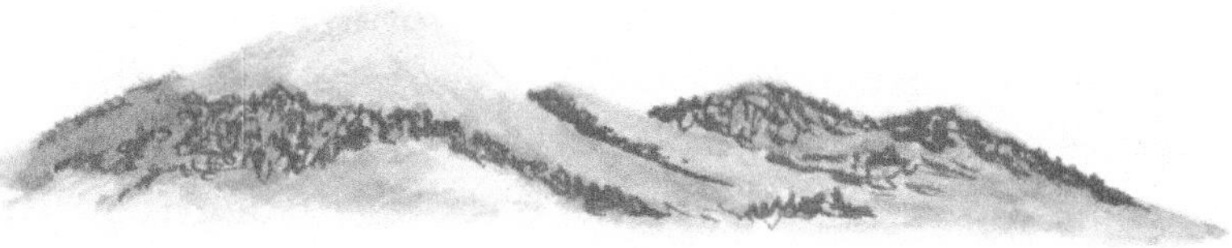

CHAPTER EIGHT

Wren had scarcely disappeared into the early morning mist with Vestie in tow, when Kyle descended Zettie's front steps and ambled slowly through her gate. Lost in thought over the myriad contradictions that surrounded The Cove, Kyle paid little heed to the direction his steps turned. The fresh pastures edging the dirt track, the fragrance wafting from blackberry bushes in bloom, failed to penetrate his awareness. Sunlight was beginning to flood The Cove but Kyle's expression was dark, overshadowed by his brooding suspicion that essential knowledge was being withheld from him, perhaps deliberately. By whom? Mistrust of The Cove, both people and place, rasped his nerves.

Startled by a sharp bark, Kyle jumped and looked up to find a border collie barring his way. The black and white canine stood its ground, not snarling but definitely keeping Kyle a safe distance from a flock of sheep crossing the road.

"Starlin, hold!" a man commanded. Kyle recognized one of the Garonflo brothers striding toward him. Was it Freeman or Hall? Kyle frowned, embarrassed he didn't remember which.

"Hall," said the gray-haired man, holding out a callused hand to Kyle. Kyle took it, but his grin faltered as his fingers were nearly crushed. Hall might appear elderly but his grip was bullish, as if he was rebuking Kyle for not remembering his name. The folks in The Cove had uncanny ways of reading one's mind, a trait Wren had often grumbled about.

"My dog din't mean to startle ya none, Kyle," Hall offered, "Starlin here is jest doing her job. We're movin' the flock to the pasture acrost the lane."

Kyle nodded and stepped back a respectful distance. Starlin immediately lost interest in him and returned to her task, nipping at the heels of the frisky lambs and turning the heads of determined ewes in the direction of the open gate. A ram with curling horns stood just inside the fence, watching his harem parade by.

"Cute things, ain't they?" Hall drawled affectionately.

Kyle admitted they were but he was more fascinated by the quick, decisive movements of the sheep dog. Starlin's brown eyes shifted from Hall's hands to the flock, quickly following the silent commands the man was giving him. When a stubborn yearling decided to go its own way, Starlin circled around and crouched in front of it, fixing a steady eye on the stray. Suddenly the animal changed its mind and meekly rejoined the flow.

When the gate was closed on the flock, Starlin trotted expectantly over to Hall, who praised her with a "That'll do, girl." and tossed her a stale biscuit. Swallowing the tidbit before it hit the ground, Starlin turned her golden brown eyes toward Kyle.

"This here's Kyle, girl," Hall responded to the dog's unspoken question. Starlin approached Kyle, circling him slowly, sniffing his jeans and boots before sitting down regally before him. She proffered a paw which Kyle solemnly accepted.

"Hain't got no need to talk, do she?" Hall chuckled.

"Oh, she talks alright," Kyle said, "just doesn't use English." Kyle glanced across the road toward the Garanflo brothers' cabin. "Freeman around?"

"Gone over to Jonah's. The professor wanted him to learn Hershall Lincoln a thing or two 'bout dog trainin'."

"*Dog* training?"

"Welp, seems like Hershall inherited a pack of hounds from his Pa and they've taken to drivin' the neighbors' cows crazy. Nothin' worse than half-trained huntin' dogs," Hall groused.

"Unless it's a sorry varmint of a boy," Kyle muttered.

"Could be Freeman will be doin' some trainin' with both dogs and boy," Hall said dryly as he rubbed his hands over his grizzled chin.

"Ah, ha!" Kyle snorted as things fell into place. He had wondered how the Cove folk would manage to take Hershall off Vestie's hands for the day. And he heartily agreed that the boy needed more "whuppin into shape" than his dogs.

Hall studied Kyle's tight features. "Fer a bright mornin', you're lookin' almighty low, son. Headin' somewheres?"

Kyle hesitated briefly, his need for answers warring with his native caution. "Not really," he admitted, "just waiting for Wren to get back."

"Where *is* that woman of yourn?"

Kyle frowned, wondering who knew what about the mysteries of The Cove. Should he say something about Wren and Vestie going to The Spring? He probed Hall's faded blue eyes and finally just shrugged. "Off up The Cove a ways." Hall gave Kyle a quick nod and then turned back to his flock who were lingering by the fence, plainly expecting some feed to materialize in the empty trough.

Watching Hall empty a pail of grain into the low bin, Kyle struggled to contain the feelings that were threatening to overflow even his habitual reserve. Who could he trust? How much dare he reveal?

Kyle frowned, muttering to himself, "Everything seems to run along so normally when you're here in the Cove until wham!" Kyle's boot cracked against a convenient fence post.

Hall put down his pail and leaned back against the fence, head cocked inquiringly.

Kyle looked up sheepishly, "Well, you have to admit that it can really shake a person up when time seems to...well, sort of, what? Run on two different tracks? Tracks that don't connect the Cove with the rest of the world?"

"So, somethin' happened when you got back to Laurel Spring last month?" Hall asked mildly.

Kyle rubbed his hands over his face. "Yeh, something happened all right. When we reached our truck, we found a bunch of flowers we left there looking almost as fresh as when I had picked them...six days earlier. Then we got back to Laurel Spring and I found Billy closing up the gas station to take his family to a Memorial Day celebration that was four days past, or so we thought! Then a busybody neighbor of ours, Brazilia, asked Wren why we came home so soon... yet our bodies carried bruises that were four, five days old! Nothing but nothing added up! Miz. Brazilia acted like we'd only been gone three days or so."

Kyle paused, trying to control his rising anger, "How do you think it felt to believe a week had passed? Hell! to *know* a week had passed, and find it was only a couple days...out there? Like we had just fallen asleep that first night on the trail, dreamt everything that happened in The Cove (both of us having the exact *same* dream!), and wake up to it being just the next day. But it wasn't... yet it was! Jesus, Hall, what happens? *Something* is going on here!

"And I don't mean like...like Brigadoon, either. Life goes on here in The Cove and it's connected with the "outside" all the time but...." Kyle threw up his hands. "And you know what eats at me the most? No one told us anything about this ... just left us to bumble around like a couple of idiots. I don't like being made a fool of... or used for someone's amusement, either!" Kyle gripped the fence rail and took a couple deep breaths, struggling to control his rising anger.

Hall leaned forward. "You're not stupid, Kyle. Think now! How could anyone tell you about this "time thing" until you had experienced it for yourself? Would you have believed 'em?"

Kyle pulled on his nose, narrowed his eyes and muttered, "Something's happened here, hasn't it? I don't know what and I don't know when but *something* definitely happened, something that's affected the relationship of 'Cove time' to 'out there'."

"It's not fer me to tell you all about it, Kyle, but I kin mebbe point you in the right direction. You've heard tell of the Borderlands, right?" Kyle nodded and Hall asked softly, "Have you figured out yet where they might be? Where you 'cross through'?"

Kyle narrowed his eyes, his mind working swiftly as he replayed events from the first time he and Wren had encountered the Cove. He slowly turned to stare down the trail that had led them into The Cove. Kyle glanced at Hall questioningly but the older man merely looked back at him, impassive, waiting.

Kyle felt like there was a hand on his back, pushing, and his anger flared. He dug in his heels. He hated not knowing what he was walking into but something was drawing him back to the Bentley place where he and Wren had first met up with Mencie, something that he couldn't resist.

With a sigh, Kyle pushed off from the fence and began walking. Hall nodded to himself and headed back to his sheep shed.

The track Kyle followed gradually narrowed until he was threading a shaded path. He reached the clearing where he and Wren had camped their first night in The Cove. Kyle paused before pushing through some briar bushes that seemed to fence off a grassy area shaded by young poplars, walnuts, and buckeyes.

There was a spring not far from the ruins of a burnt out cabin where Kyle found a tin cup he and Wren had left there. Refreshed by the cold water, Kyle studied the standing stones barely visible among the rank weeds. He was tired but it didn't feel right to sit on those old tomb stones.

Instead he walked over to the flat rock that had once been the door sill of the cabin and gratefully eased down on it. Resting his head in his hands, Kyle basked in the warm sun, lulled by the buzzing of countless bees around the clover. He felt himself relaxing, his tensions seeping down into the threshold now supporting him.

Surrendering to the warmth, Kyle was soon drifting, the border between sleep and wakefulness blurring. Kyle chose not to fight the spell-like tendrils invading his spirit. He had been here before. The air shimmered with shapes flickering at the edge of his vision, shapes that slowly resolved into images of his hunted ancestors. Once again he saw the gaunt warriors, alert and wary; the women herding frightened children; elders checking the path behind them with quick, furtive glances. He smelled their fear...and thrilled at their defiance!

Their time was running out and they knew it. The army scouts were closing in. How much longer could they elude discovery? Would they have enough time to reach the haven offered by The Cove? Something clicked in Kyle's mind. Time! They had had no time, yet he knew they had somehow escaped capture. *Time!* This was the key. Something or someone had gained for them the time they needed.

Kyle's right leg was cramping and tingling. He wanted to stand up, but he could not bring himself to move. He felt glued to that threshold, numb, powerless to resist what he knew was coming. He did not have long to wait.

A pall-like silence descended. No bird chirped, no bee buzzed by, not even a breeze stirred the leaves. Sweating profusely now, Kyle stared at the sunbaked ground between his legs, watching it absorb the droplets falling from his forehead. His throat was parched and dry. Just when he thought he could bear it no longer, the coolness of the spirit world overshadowed him. Kyle shivered. For *him*, time had run out.

Slowly Kyle raised his eyes to meet the piercing gaze of the Ancient One looming over him. As before, that regal, ravaged face filled his sight, the deep, all-seeing eyes penetrating Kyle's defenses and posing the questions from which Kyle had run, time and time again. No more! His time was up; his bargaining over.

Stunned, shamed, Kyle bowed his head. His loose white hair fell forward, baring his neck. He could see the tattered moccasins of the Elder, toe to toe with his own boots. It was Time that he accept the consequences of all his previous choices. From the moment Crowe had died, Kyle had tried to hold time back, even as it continued to flow around him. Now the game was up; he was caught.

Kyle drew a shuddering breath and dared to look up again into the face of the Ancient One. His fingers tightened on the stone threshold as he mouthed the "yes" he had withheld for so long. Even as he did so, the Ancient One began to dissolve into the shimmering light surrounding him until only the stern face remained sharply defined. Kyle's heart stopped. Had he waited too long? By refusing to accept the role that had passed to him with his twin's death, Kyle had hoped to somehow keep his brother at his side...and possibly, to bring him back. What a desperate farce! Was his "yes" too late now?

He dropped his chin to his chest. "I'm sorry," he whispered agonizingly, "I'm sorry I was so stupid, such a, a coward." Only silence greeted his confession. Slowly Kyle raised his eyes, confused.

Panic started to nibble at his heart as Kyle waited through an interminable moment until he saw a nod of acceptance from the Ancient One and the slow smile that signaled his forgiveness. His body tingled when he heard the harsh accents of his secret name and mission: Echota!

No one knew what had passed to him while he had stood at Crowe's death bed, not even his father. His father's parting words to Kyle's dying twin had been transmuted into a mission for Kyle, a commission he had refused to accept. If God was taking his twin, He would not find a willing servant in Kyle! Now Kyle breathed deeply, drawing his first free breath since he had begun his self-defeating feud with God.

The Ancient One touched Kyle's shoulders. A shaman's mantle, woven of myriad bird feathers, settled lightly on the one for whom it was intended. Silently Kyle asked himself why he had run from this for so long? At last, time was ticking for him again and he could feel changes, long delayed, begin within himself.

As his normal vision returned, Kyle surveyed the now empty clearing. A number of disconnected truths bumped around in his head and heart; facts which touched on his deepest identity, his mission and his calling; truths which he now knew, connected him directly with the mystery that was The Cove.

He had wandered out here, seeking answers but had only found larger questions. His perplexity over the bizarre relationship of time in The Cove to time in the "outer world" had only deepened and become far too personal! He had wanted to figure things out for himself. All he knew now was that he had to (once again) cry "uncle" and seek the help he had spurned. With a rueful grin, Kyle stood up, stretched, and began the long walk to Jonah's house.

As he strode up the road, Kyle replayed the insights which had just come to him, trying to fit them into what he already knew about the history of The Cove and his people. He *had* to find out what had happened, not only to The Cove people but to his own as well.

However, if he was given answers, he would not only have to accept but use powers he had once refused. His fists clenched and unclenched. Not knowing made him feel vulnerable to manipulation, something he abhorred. Was he being used by these strange people who so jealously guarded the mystery that was Lovada Cove?

As Kyle turned off the main road onto the well-worn path that led to Jonah's house, he studied the stone structure bristling with antennae, satellite dishes and solar panels. The low hum of generators mingled with the humming of bees flitting back and forth from hives set near the woods behind the house. The paradoxes in the scene highlighted the questions that clashed within Kyle's mind.

Jonah's door stood open and Kyle strolled through without knocking. The stocky man was sitting with his back to the door, wholly concentrated on the computer screen flickering in front of him. He glanced up when Kyle's boots scuffed across the floor and waved him to a chair.

"Give me a minute here to close out and I'll be with you. Was expecting you, son," Jonah rumbled through his white beard. "I told Freeman to take Hershall out to see how a well-trained dog pack works together. He's got no control over hisn'."

Ironically, knowing he was expected only added fuel to Kyle's confused anger. He refused to take the proffered seat and instead, wandered around the low-ceilinged room which was lined with books dealing with everything from theology to solar energy. An old ledger, open on the table, caught his attention and without asking, Kyle picked it up. He was leafing through it when Jonah swung around from the fading screen. Just as Kyle started to put the book down, some familiar names caught his eye. Sweat popped out on his brow and his hands shook.

"Find something?" Jonah inquired, when he noticed Kyle's distress. "That ledger is the oldest burial record we have, dates back to the 1790's. We usually keep it in the chapel but I brought it over here to enter the data into a program I'm working on."

Kyle grunted, snapped the brittle pages shut and narrowed his eyes. "The Cherokee names in there – I, they, well, um, they're familiar. Were *my* people among those who found refuge back here? And...and who, well, died here?"

Jonah drew a deep breath. "Back in the 1830's, some of the Cherokee did make it back in here. And a few stayed on. You'd know your family names better than I, Kyle."

Kyle hesitated, suspicions coursing through him. His eyes were rueful when he looked back at Jonah. "I've come here looking for answers but now, I'm not so sure I want them."

Jonah nodded compassionately and gestured once more to the straight-back chair. Kyle grabbed it, flipped it around, and sat down, resting his elbows on its back. He licked his dry lips. "I went over to the Bentley place this morning because I suspected that's where Wren and I "crossed over" or "through" or whatever happens when people enter Cove time." Kyle paused, searching for words.

Jonah said nothing, waiting for Kyle to reveal how much he'd figured out.

"I- I learned a few things there," Kyle said softly, his anger collapsing. "Jonah, I thought this "time thing" as you folks call it, was like a doorway, a threshold that a person crosses...but there's more to it, isn't there?"

"Much more," Jonah responded, as he eyed the younger man who was staring deep within himself.

"Exactly what are you searching for, Kyle?" Jonah asked softly but sternly. "Are you looking to just satisfy your curiosity? Beware, Kyle. Is it facts you want or do you want the Truth behind them, the meaning and purpose of this admittedly strange interaction of Cove time with time "out there"? The full story is...," Jonah scratched the full white beard hiding his lips, "the full truth is like the Word ... 'living and effective, sharper than any two-edged sword, penetrating and dividing soul and spirit, judging the heart....'," Jonah paused, assessing Kyle who was listening with clenched jaws, hands raised as if to ward off danger.

The scream of a distant red-tail hawk as it circled prey, pierced the silence. "Hebrews, chapter four," Kyle muttered as if strangling. He swallowed and painfully continued the passage, "Nothing is concealed from him; all lies bare and exposed to the eyes of the one to whom we must render an account." A Silence filled the cabin as Kyle clutched the chair back, staring at unseen images.

"Well, which is it, Kyle?" Jonah said finally.

Kyle rubbed his hands across his eyes. "I need the Truth, Jonah. God knows... yes, *God* knows I've run from it long enough. No more. I...can't...run...anymore."

"You have earned the right to the full story, Kyle, the whole Truth," Jonah said quietly, "but I'm not the man to tell you. You have to go to the Lore-Keepers."

"You mean Bewley and Haidia?" Kyle asked, remembering the time Mencie had taken him, along with Wren, to visit an elderly couple whose cabin stood deep in The Cove. "Why them?" Kyle asked, mystified. "Can't you tell me? Or don't you know, either?"

"I know what I need to know," Jonah said soberly. "But I suspect that there are parts of the story that only you, you and Wren, should know for they are concerned with you in some way."

Kyle suddenly turned pale, so pale that Jonah jumped up and stepped quickly to his side. Before Kyle could catch his breath to object, the older man laid his hands on Kyle's silvery hair, stroking the sweat-darkened headband. No words passed through Jonah's lips but power flowed into Kyle, strong and comforting. After a few minutes, Kyle reached up and ran his fingers over the white hairs curling on the back of Jonah's big hands.

"It's time. Are you ready?" Jonah asked softly. Kyle nodded and rose slowly to his feet

"Wait for Wren," Jonah decreed and Kyle smiled briefly, grateful for the short respite this offered him. He straightened the band holding back his hair and ran his hands over his face, as if resettling his normal stoical façade. It wasn't his style to let others, even Wren, see that he wasn't in full control of himself.

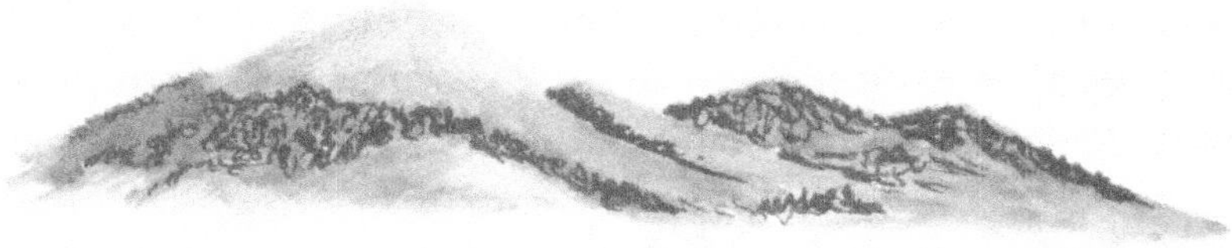

CHAPTER NINE

Kyle was munching a sandwich, his feet up on the rail of Zettie's porch, when he caught sight of Wren and Vestie ambling across the meadow. Wren looked diminutive beside Vestie's slender height. They were laughing, leaning toward one another affectionately. When Wren caught sight of Kyle, she waved and then hugged Vestie who turned up the road toward Oma's place. Wren skipped lightly up Zettie's porch steps and dropped her empty backpack.

Kyle watched Wren's exhilaration slowly change to bewilderment as she toed the limp canvas. "Kyle... Kyle?" she paused, licking her lips. "There's so much I wanted to tell you but it's fading!"

Kyle's boots hit the floor with a thump as he turned toward Wren, puzzled and uncertain of her meaning. "Say what?"

"The hours spent at the Spring today...they're slipping away like a dream when you wake up." Wren wrapped her arms around herself, surprised and troubled. "I can't recall anything about what Vestie and I said or did... at least, not explicitly. There's just a hazy impression that it was a good experience and that some important things happened which affected Vestie."

Wren leaned against the porch rail, running her fingers through her hair in exasperation. "It wasn't like this when *we* left the Spring, was it, Kyle?" Curious but cautious, Kyle said nothing but simply waited as Wren groped her way toward understanding what was happening to her. "I feel like I know things now that I didn't know before Vestie and I went to the Spring, things that could, possibly *will*, come back to me if or when I need them. But right now, all I can recall are my own feelings."

"Which are?" Kyle prompted.

"I felt so, so alive! And cleansed and freer than I've ever been. It's much like what I felt after you and I went to the Spring ... but with a difference. This time was for Vestie more than for me. This time I was more of a mediator rather than a receiver. Not that I didn't benefit personally, too." Wren laughed lightly and swung around to face the late afternoon sun.

Kyle watched his wife silently, unwilling to break in on Wren's fragile joy, a joy he envied but could not share. Unbeknownst to herself, Wren was radiant. Her blue-green eyes were luminous and her hair, windblown and tousled, glowed in the late afternoon sun. When Wren leaned over to kiss Kyle, he jerked back as if fearing her touch. Startled, Wren paused, noticing for the first time the shadows pooled in Kyle's dark eyes. Her radiance dimmed and pained surprise flared in its place.

Immediately contrite, Kyle reached for her, pulling her into his lap. "Sorry, honey," he muttered, "I didn't mean that as a rejection. It's just... been a rough day, I guess."

While Wren held herself stiff and contained in his arms, Kyle smoothed her reddish curls and murmured, "I wish you could see yourself just now. You looked like a princess of the sun as you came across the meadow with Vestie. So joy-filled and lovely...so different from what *I* feel... ." Kyle tried to smile but his lips felt stiff.

Cupping Kyle's face in her hands, Wren studied him earnestly. "What happened while I was gone, Kyle? Who did you meet up with?"

Kyle stared across the meadow, averting his face from Wren's anxious eyes. He was torn. He wanted to shield Wren from the fears gnawing at him and yet he desperately needed to share them with her.

"Kyle?" Wren whispered, prodding.

"I'm here, honey," he responded, squeezing her hands between his own. Drawing in a deep breath, Kyle plunged into unknown waters. "I –I need you."

Wren was alarmed. Never before had her self-sufficient husband ever admitted *that*. What had happened? Her concern deepening, Wren touched Kyle's cheek gently, probing for the hurt or fear she knew was there.

Kyle continued to stare into the distance and his silence frightened Wren even more. "Kyle? You've got to tell me. Is there something I can do?"

"Just come with me," Kyle whispered in a tight voice. "Come with me to see the Lore Keepers."

Wren sucked in her breath. "Bewley and Haidia?"

"Yes. They will explain about what happens to time whenever anyone visits The Cove."

Wren shivered as she reached for Kyle's hands. They were cold, clammy. She clutched them against her chest, breathing warmly on them and kissing them before she slipped from her husband's knees.

"Well, what are we waiting for?" she asked as she untied the sweater from around her waist and pushed her arms through the sleeves. The evening air was suddenly chill. Kyle swallowed the last of the tea from the mug beside his chair and rose stiffly. His obvious reluctance bothered Wren. What could he possibly dread so?

"Zettie knows where we're going," Kyle said, answering Wren's unspoken question. "In fact, she gave me a basket to return to Haidia, filled with some of her baking."

Wren's lips twitched. "You DO know that you shouldn't return anything to a neighbor empty? It's more than just bad manners. You risk ending a relationship," she explained softly as Kyle picked up the cloth-draped hamper.

"Guess we'd better not nibble on that short bread then," Kyle remarked, as he reached for Wren's hand.

"She'd *know*," Wren warned solemnly as they began to thread their way along a shady path that led from Zettie's back yard, across a branch that rippled down the slope and into the woods separating Bewley and Haidia's place from the rest of The Cove.

Ten minutes later, they were ducking under the shapely evergreens that stood sentinel around a dark brown cabin nestled almost invisibly in their shade. Neither Kyle nor Wren were surprised to find Bewley and Haidia waiting for them on their pleasant, screened porch. The Dean purred in a late beam of sunshine warming the steps. Instinctively, Kyle looked around. He had noted that whenever the grey cat appeared, Mencie generally showed up, too.

"Bet they'll say they were expecting us and are just waiting for Mencie," Kyle muttered under his breath as Wren ran swiftly up the steps into Haidia's welcoming embrace. Kyle shrugged off his pique over the Cove's mysterious relay system and solemnly returned Bewley's handshake and Haidia's hug.

The petite elder patted her neatly coiled braids and waved toward the table where a hand-carved bowl of fresh peaches rested. "These are the last ones for this year," Bewley beamed proudly as he limped over to Kyle to take Zettie's basket from him. Wren rolled the fruit appreciatively in her hand before biting in. With juice spurting down her chin, she savored its full-bodied sweetness.

"They look mighty good, Bewley," Kyle observed, "I didn't think you could grow peaches around here."

"Tain't easy," the old man admitted, as he eased himself into a wicker chair, liberally stuffed with cushions. Using his other foot, Bewley pushed his twisted leg closer to the chair.

Watching him, Kyle wondered when and how the old man had been injured.

Haidia distracted Kyle's thoughts (deliberately?) by announcing proudly, "Bewley, he growed them peach trees hisself, takin' pits from some fruit we found on an old tree here. Planted them where they'd git mornin' sun and be protected from the worst of the cold in winter."

"Even so, we don't get a crop every year," Bewley admitted. "Depends on when we git the last frost. Blackberry winter kin kill the blossoms afore the fruit is set."

Kyle nodded absently, not particularly interested in peach culture. His eyes wandered aimlessly over the cheerful porch until he felt Wren shift beside him on the swing. Mencie was coming down the path, gray poncho flapping along with her broad-brimmed hat. Her golden eyes glimmered as she caressed The Dean who arched his back into her hand when she reached the steps.

"Was waitin' on ya, Mencie," Haidia called out and Kyle grunted in satisfaction at being on target about *something* for a change. Wren poked him in the ribs and he grinned slightly, knowing she had read his thoughts. Distractedly, he plucked a peach from the bowl and was soon involved in adjusting his ideas about paradise.

Mencie also reached for a peach and deftly twisted it to remove the pit, then settled into a rocker. For awhile, Kyle heard nothing but the creak of the old chairs and the slurp of people savoring the lush fruit. "This is what a peach is meant to be like," he mused, wondering how long it was since he'd last enjoyed tree-ripened fruit. Glancing down at Wren, he was tempted to lean over and lick the juice sweetening her lips. Just then, she flicked her eyes up at him and Kyle read a matching desire. Kyle's shoulders relaxed a fraction.

Bewley chuckled, his weathered face cross-hatched with small wrinkles. But slowly his expression sobered and Kyle felt him readying himself to continue the story of The Cove's early years he had begun during Kyle and Wren's first visit to The Cove earlier in the spring. Wiping his hands on the damp cloth Haidia passed over, Bewley peered at the younger man whose Cherokee ancestry was written across his broad facial features and coarse, prematurely greyed hair.

"The Trail of Tears," Bewley intoned and a chill ran up Kyle's back.

"Thet's what they call it now, don't they?" Bewley mused. "But there's more than *one* trail in the story, ain't there? You heerd 'bout them, din'tcha, Kyle?"

"Every child on the Boundary knows the stories of what happened around 1838," Kyle responded cautiously.

"Likely," Bewley affirmed agreeably, leaning back and carefully stretching his legs out before him. "But they's parts that none knows but a few."

No one on the porch but the Dean moved. He leapt lightly onto Mencie's lap and circled until his tail was wrapped comfortably around him. When he settled, his purring formed a soft background to Bewley's drawl.

"As you know," the elder observed, "not ever'body in the tribes showed up when Gen'ral Winfield Scott put out the call for your people to come into the removal forts. Fact is, a fair number of you'n's lit back into these here mountains, follerin' trails only they knew."

Bewley looked sharply at Kyle's shadowed eyes and impassive face. "Reckon you could name me some of 'em," he commented but didn't wait for Kyle to acknowledge or dispute the fact. But Wren sucked in her breath as she felt Kyle stiffen beside her.

"Them soldiers, they had look-outs up on Watch Mountain in Tennessee so some of your people who had slipped away could only travel at night and hide out durin'
the day. The women carried weapons bundled in their skirts while the men scouted ahead. They'd send word back and then someone would lead the women and childern to the next

hidey hole. They was some whites that helped by passin' them food or lettin' them stay in their houses or barns durin' the day. But they were others who let on to the soldiers if'n they see'd a group of Cherokee passin' by."

Kyle lowered his eyes and studied his clenched hands.

"So, along the way, more of yore folks got picked up by the soldiers and sent back to the corrals. Hardly none of'em put up a fight – just weren't their way. They was really a peaceable folk. And civilized, too. Fact is, most of'em could read and write their own language, thanks to Chief Sequoya who had worked out a kind of syllabary for them to use. Why even parts of the Bible was already wrote down in Cherokee. It made no kind of sense to them that the gov'mint that claimed itself Christian would go back on treaties they'd signed with the tribe...."

"Bewley," Haidia interrupted softly. "Don't you reckon Kyle here knows all about that? No point in gettin' all lathered up and tellin' *him* what the the Tsalagi was like and how bad they was treated!"

Bewley coughed apologetically, "Guess ah'm sort of preaching to the choir, ain't I?"

Kyle waved off Bewley's words of apology with a grin, "Hey, anyone who is for us, can't be against us." He felt Wren stir at his side when she heard him casually refer to the Cherokee as "us", something he had carefully avoided doing for years.

"Yup, well to git on with it," Bewley picked up, "they was a bunch of Cherokee, led by one of the old shamans, what managed to slip eastward along a trail known only to the shamans 'cause it led down to the holy places by the hot springs. But this time, the leaders turned off from that trail long about where Lovada Branch crossed over it and were follerin' the branch up a gully round Unaka Mountain when one of the soldiers from Scott's army got wind of 'em. He roused up a bunch of volunteers to go in after 'em."

"That shaman, he was one of their important leaders," Bewley noted, "Seems he figured if he could get his people back to Lovada Cove, there'd be a chancet fer 'em."

Kyle narrowed his eyes. "Why'd he think that? What was so special about The Cove?"

Bewley leaned back and cocked his head slightly, sensing he was being tested. How much did Kyle know or guess by now? Like all good story tellers, Bewley liked to have an element of surprise in his tale and preferred not to show his hand before he was ready. But Kyle, too, was playing his game close to his chest so Bewley couldn't fathom what cards he already held.

Haidia broke in. "Lots of Cherokee had passed through Lovada Cove over time, Kyle. Whites had settled back here more than a hunnerd year before. Some folks say they wouldn't have survived a 'tall weren't it fer the help them Cherokee giv'em early on. Some of 'em even married in..."

"So they done, Maw," Bewley broke in. "Reckon it was some of their descendants that spoke up at the church meetin' when Wasituna (he was one of the boys what escaped Col. Thomas over at Noland's Branch in Tennessee) sneaked in to ast if his folk could hide out in the Cove fer a bit."

Bewley glanced Kyle's way and was pleased to see him sitting back now, arms crossed on his chest, listening intently and nodding occasionally when Bewley's tale agreed with what he had been taught by his elders.

"The way it's told here," Bewley emphasized, "the Cove folks decided to take in ever'one as could make it back here. One of the women offered to lead 'em on back to the Spring itself. No one would *ever* find'em there 'cause no one knew where it was 'cept..." Bewley stopped when he heard Wren's startled hiss and saw her eyes flash.

Haidia leaned over and patted Wren's knee. "The Keeper of the Spring" was a Cherokee woman back then," she said softly. "They had guarded the Spring long before us whites ever walked up here...and I guess you could say they still do. If'n you'd look back fer enuf in yore family, you'd find at least one of your mamaws was Cherokee." Wren tilted her head, frowning but interested.

"So then," Bewley resumed, "some of our people were leadin' in a band of Cherokee but had only got'em as far as the church house when word come that the "volunteer" soldiers (bounty hunters is what they really was) had follered them as fur as the Bentley place. Some men from the Cove went out to parley with'em a bit to gain that extry bit o'time that was needed to git all the Cherokee safely hid away at the Spring."

Bewley looked down and sighed gently when Kyle broke in, "It didn't work well, did it? Your men were killed when they wouldn't tell what they knew." Bewley nodded sadly as Kyle continued, "So that is where it happened! I heard that story years ago and again when Wren and I were ..." Kyle stopped abruptly and shook his head, checking what he was about to reveal.

"Go on, Bewley," he urged instead, "My people never told me exactly where all this happened. I doubt that many of them even know after all these years. There were a few that did though ...like my father."

Bewley looked up eagerly, "He a shaman?"

"Was," Kyle said sharply. "It's...it's passed to me but Pa died before he could tell me all he knew. The truth is he'd been training..." Kyle paused, and swallowed painfully, grateful for Wren's firm grasp of his hand. "He'd been training my brother, Crowe, because he was the elder. But Crowe and I were so close...three minutes birth time isn't much of a difference," he said with a bark of a laugh, "that I knew most everything our Pa told him. Crowe had the Sight and understood, even when we were boys, that I would be the one who would receive the mantle, though he never actually told me so."

Haidia's eyes were moist as she leaned toward Kyle, "Losin' him must be hard, even now," she murmured gently. Kyle simply nodded, not trusting his voice to respond. Wren snuggled closer, offering him her own body warmth to ward off the chill of a death that had touched Kyle so nearly.

Bewley cleared his throat, "Did they tell you that when them "irregulars" suspected we was hidin' the Cherokee they was trailin', they shot our men right on the spot when they refused to lead them in? The soldiers left sayin' they'd be back in force to kill ever' single man, woman and child in the Cove if we din't give up them Cherokee."

Haidia picked up the story sadly, "Folks in The Cove had heard the shots and come runnin' but 'twas too late. One of the men lived just long enough to warn them that more soldiers was comin' back. Folks carried the bodies back to their homes where the women washed their men – they was three of 'em – and dressed 'em and covered their faces with cloths dipped in camphor to keep 'em from turnin' brown. One by one they were taken into the church and laid out in the sanctuary. "

"Both men and women went to work diggin' hasty graves...din't have time to make no coffins even. Ever'one came in to comfort the families and pray with 'em, even the Cherokee who hadn't yet been takin' to the Spring. They was all prayin', not knowin' what to do 'cause there weren't no time left to save the Cherokee still hidden in The Cove."

"Time had run out fer 'em," Bewley broke in grimly. "It was lookin' mighty bleak right then. No one wanted to die nor see their kin kilt but it looked like it was comin' to thet ..."

Bewley continued in a harsh whisper, "Now, what ah'm about to tell you is God's holy truth." He paused, gazing out into the gathering dusk as if reliving the scene. He swiped at the tears threatening to spill down his seamed cheeks and Kyle wondered if one of the dead men had been an ancestor of Bewley or possibly a relative much loved and still mourned?

Bewley cleared his throat, "Seems like without any of 'em in the church noticin' it, the air had cooled and a thick mist was a'creepin' up the Cove. The old shaman, he was standin' at the church door, lookin' down the road with his hands raised, almost like he was callin' it up. Ever' one was suddenly real quiet, even the squallin' babies."

Kyle felt Wren lean closer when Bewley asked, "You know how voices kin carry in a heavy fog? Things kin seem close and far at the same time? Welp, seems like all too soon, ever'one in that church could hear those soldiers comin'; could hear everthin' they was sayin', could even hear the jingle of the horses' bridles. Then it sounded like them boys was fixin' bayonets to their rifles.

"Thet there shaman, he jest stayed where he was in the doorway, not sayin' nothing, not even movin'. Seemed like no one in the church was even breathin' as they heerd them army boys ride right past the church, actin' like they didn't see it a'tall. They jest kept on agoin' into that mist and not one of'em ever found a single person in The Cove. Seems like they never even caught sight of any of the houses or farms or fields! Leastways they din't do a thang anywheres in The Cove."

Bewley added with a sly chuckle, "Fact is, it took'em a turrible long time to find their way back home, cause they jest got all turned around in that-there mist. By the time they hooked up with Gen'ral Scott agin not one of'em was the least bit interested in chasin' down Cherokee here abouts nor anywhere else in these mountains. Seemed down right narvous whenever it grew onto dusk..."

Kyle felt Wren quivering beside him. A chill had crept over him, too. He asked softly, warily, "That's still known to happen, isn't it." He stared at Mencie, who sat fixed like a grey monument on the porch seat with only her golden eyes gleaming in her ageless face. Wisps of fog were even now rolling along the ground as evening fell.

Haidia rose and lit the lantern hanging from a chain but even its golden glow didn't dispel the eeriness Kyle felt. He looked up as Bewley cleared his throat.

"Meanwhile back at the church...," Wren quipped nervously, in an attempt to dispel the jitters that were nipping her nerves.

"Yuh'm, well when nothin' more happened," Bewley continued, "the shaman stepped back from the door. He took the hand of a young Cherokee woman who had come into the church with him and together they walked up to where them three dead men was laid out.

"The shaman put a hand to the bier and said to the folks gathered there, 'These men died for lack of time. In dyin' they saved my people. Darkness is falling over our tribal lands now. The Spirit Ones, the Ukdena, will remain but will not be understood by most of the folk that are left. But here, where white blood was spilled to save us, some of us will always remain and the Ukdena will protect this Cove.'

"Turnin' to the solemn girl at his side, he said somethin' in Cherokee. Later folks figured it was somethin' like, 'Daughter, will you agree to be a Warder of the Borderlands in gratitude for the sacrifice of these people?'

When she laid her hand over her heart and nodded, the shaman took her hand and placed it over the heart of each of the dead men in turn. To the people watching, he said, 'She will be your guardian and will patrol the borders from henceforth.'"

"Then she said to the Cove folk," Bewley resumed, 'I am your daughter and a daughter of the Tsalagi. I will do this until another comes to take my place.'"

"The shaman added," Bewley whispered, watching Kyle closely "that never again would there be a lack of time here. Time itself would now serve to protect The Cove. Since then, the Cove has been held within the Mysteries of the spirit world. Only those who are meant to find it, do. Those who do, come and go freely, unremarked by the outer world. The time they spend here does not register on any calendar. The mists forever surround this valley, protecting the life here, even as those men protected the Tsalagi.

When the Shaman lifted the camphor soaked cloths from the faces of the dead men... why they looked as if age had never touched them. We knew they had found that fullness of time for which we are all destined."

Kyle's body sagged against the back of the swing he shared with Wren. He understood now. Oh yes, he understood. Here was one of the few places in the world where everything and everyone was in right relationship. Those who sought The Cove but who were not in harmony with its purposes would never find it. In fact, *couldn't* find it. So he had been taught by the elders but Kyle had ceased to believe there were any places left where such balance existed. His belief had collapsed with the death of Crowe.

Kyle felt Mencie's eyes upon him and looked up. Once before he had glimpsed the fair Cherokee maiden she had been. Time had taken its toll but slowly and gently with this generous woman. Mencie was literally ageless but now she was tired and her charge was coming to an end. Another was being readied and already some of Mencie's power was slipping away. That was why Porter had been able to come so close to betraying The Cove.

Only Wren's choice, supported by the prayer of all the Cove members, had thwarted that catastrophe. An unsought but inescapable truth now assailed Kyle. He and Wren were meant to be the bridge for a mysterious change of power taking place in The Cove.

Beyond the glowing light of the porch, a thick mist slowly wrapped itself around the little cabin. As Kyle stared directly into Mencie's golden eyes, he heard half-forgotten words proclaimed within his head. *"Let us cherish a vision of a world so enlightened and beauteous, that it shall come to be."*

Like a rose unfolding finally and inevitably, teachings Kyle had received as a boy on the Boundary, now achieved blazing maturity. If he truly believed and accepted that everything and everyone was related, that he must ceaselessly strive to be in right relationship with all around him – it followed, simply and clearly, that the resonance of his most intimate thoughts and actions today would shape the world's tomorrows. So simple, so true but so far from fulfillment!

Kyle felt the eyes of all those on the porch focused on him, not probing or judging but simply encouraging. The burden of anger and regret which had drained his soul's energies was dissolving in the love and acceptance of these strange good people who accepted his burden as their own.

At the edges of the meager glow from the lantern, other eyes glimmered in the mist and Kyle was reminded of the terrible night on the mountain when Wren had faced her ultimate test. What had saved her then were the praying presences that hovered in the dark storm-lashed forest surrounding them – the Cove members that Zettie had sent to watch over her.

Now it was Kyle's turn to be the focus of their wordless love and gentle power. Wren, sitting quietly beside him, was also asking to share his burden and his call. What had seemed an impossible vocation to Kyle, one he had rejected and run from all his life, now felt not only bearable but actually desirable, for Kyle had finally found his one and only right path. It was a path of beauty which, if pursued with purpose and care in his heart, would ultimately lead to a world-embracing kinship.

Feeling Wren shift beside him, Kyle turned and in the depths of her eyes saw a mirror of his own soul. Astonishingly, miraculously, he understood that Wren was sharing in all the revelations that were flooding his own spirit! As he finally gave up his stubborn attempt to hold on to Crowe, the twin who had been the half of his soul for the first eighteen years of his life, Kyle received a new gift. By accepting the loss of what he had never been meant to keep, Kyle was enabled to receive the soul-mate destined to be knit even more intimately into his heart.

On that early summer night, witnessed by the solemn approval of Bewley and Haidia, Mencie and the Dean, Kyle felt himself wedded to Wren in a union that exceeded even their marriage bond. Their lives' destiny and goal was mysteriously but beyond any doubt, a shared and single ministry. Such gifts were not given without cost. Kyle slipped his arm around Wren wishing that he could spare her the ordeal he knew lay ahead for them.

Wordlessly, Wren laid her fingers on his lips and shook her head, stilling his incipient protest. He should not, could not protect her nor could she spare him from the pain that their future portended. They were part of the larger mystery that was Lovada Cove. Their time had come, with its incredible possibilities for good as well as its as yet, unnamed dangers. Wren was well and truly aware of Kyle's assent and had united her consent with his. One step of the Great Task was now complete.

The Dean on Mencie's lap lifted his head as if hearing some distant cry audible only to his keener ears. Lightly, Mencie stroked the soft grey fur that lay, all but invisible, on her worn poncho. The Dean yawned and settled himself more comfortably but in the instant before his eyes shuttered closed, Kyle and Wren glimpsed themselves mirrored in their inscrutable depths.

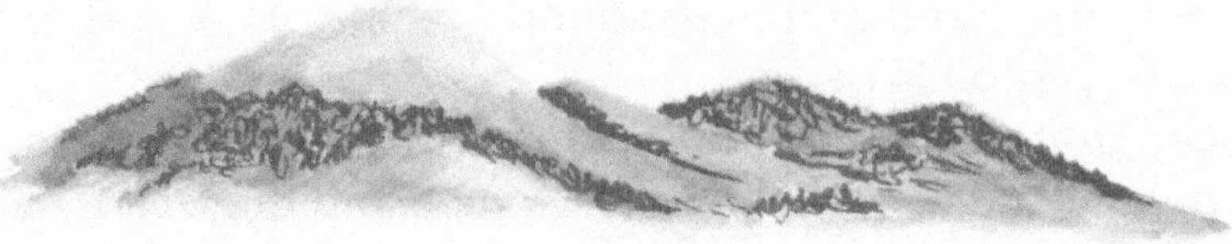

CHAPTER TEN

"Now, Maw, you cain't do thet," Locke stormed, staring down into Zettie's determined face. Kyle, who was leaning against the doorframe of the kitchen, folded his arms across his chest and grinned. Locke wasn't going to win this one. Even Zettie's thick white hair was bristling.

"I'll take nothin' off'n you, son," she tossed back. "Those pore folks need help and I can at least teach their women some English. So long as folks keep throwin' off on them 'cause they can't explain theyselves, they'll be a good many more troubles here than there needs be. And the Mexicans will be stuck tendin' land fer others until they drop. It ain't right! You know it. I know it. So I'm going back with you whether or no it's agreeable with you!"

Locke threw up his hands and barged out of the kitchen. Wren, who had also witnessed the argument, raised an eyebrow at Kyle who hastened to protest, "Now, honey, I'm just lost in admiration of your Mamaw and am thinking I'm one lucky man that you've inherited so much of her pluck."

"Yeh sure, Big Boy," Wren drawled softly and punched his arm. "Just wipe that smirky grin off your face and help us get ready to go. Zettie's stuff is already on the porch."

Just then, Vestie's sons came tearing up the road, punching and shouting at one another. Vestie's sharp voice startled them both into silence. "Hershall Glenning! Denver

Ray! Ah'm right ill at you'ns and yore argufyin', so jest you hesh up and git this wagon loaded with yore Mamaw's totes. Head on out toward the notch. Delphie and I will be along right smartly."

Wren suppressed a chuckle as the boys stopped punching each other and backed away from Vestie, eyes wide in shock. Had the kitchen stove spoken up, Wren doubted they would have been more startled. Vestie herself looked slightly surprised at the authority in her voice. When the boys' backs were turned, Wren gave her a thumb's up.

Locke swung around the corner of the house with the ash bucket he had just emptied. His eyes swept over Vestie with such frustration that Wren suspected Locke, too, had recently met up with the new Vestie. Wren mentally filed a question, intending to ask Kyle what he knew or thought about Locke's feelings for his sister-in-law.

Zettie came sweeping through the front door with a small, old-fashioned suitcase in her hand, appearing to be only half-dressed without her apron. Her blue eyes snapped as she handed the case to the reluctant Locke, directing him to load it on the two-wheeled hand-cart that would carry their gear to the notch where Locke and Kyle had parked their trucks three days earlier.

Wren discreetly signaled Kyle to fall in with her at the end of the small procession that was winding its way across the meadow. Denver Ray and Hershall were pulling the cart together but so sullenly that Wren could tell their earlier dispute was still in progress, albeit silently. Hershall, by walking slightly slower than Denver Ray, was deliberately leaving most of weight to be pulled by the younger boy who, in turn, was jerking the cart viciously against Hershall's heels.

Vestie and Mamaw Zettie were absorbed in some private conversation while Locke strode ahead of the group, still disgruntled. Delphie, who normally clung close to Vestie whenever others were around, was ranging freely through the ankle high grass, plucking various flowers and leaves that she took to Mencie who was accompanying them to the notch. The elder was not much taller than the nine year old and the bond between them seemed singularly respectful. Mencie appeared to be telling Delphie about each plant, speaking in a soft voice that was barely more than a whisper.

"Do you think Delphie understands?" Kyle asked Wren, gesturing to the two of them further ahead on the trail.

"What do you mean?"

"Well, Delphie doesn't talk and Porter never let her attend school," Kyle said impatiently, "Isn't she deaf? Or, well, simple?"

Wren was startled. "Kyle! How can you say that? Of course she can hear. And she understands far more than we *ever* will!"

"How do you know that?" Kyle asked, surprised by Wren's certitude.

Wren stopped in her tracks and cocked her head, brow furrowed. "I just do, I guess. I think, maybe at first, I wondered what was wrong with her. But there's nothing *wrong*, oh, no, far from it. She's different certainly and I don't know why she doesn't talk ... maybe she just hasn't felt the need?

Or," Wren picked her way slowly, trying to understand her own strong intuitions regarding this child who was, in truth, her half-sister. "or maybe it's been a way of protecting herself. Now that Porter's... gone, she might start talking some. She could what? Feel safe now?"

Wren looked up into Kyle's sun-browned face, hoping he could grasp what she was struggling to put into words. She was certain that Delphie's muteness was not due to a physical problem but *how* she knew that, Wren couldn't say. Until Kyle had brought up the topic of Delphie's disability, Wren had never questioned how she knew all she did about this semi-wild child. To her shock, she realized that a profound but inexplicable link bound her to Delphie, something that was more than their unacknowledged sisterhood.

Kyle focused on Delphie and Mencie thoughtfully for a while before asking Wren, "Do you think that Delphie's ears are super-sensitive? That perhaps she can hear things beyond the normal range for humans?"

"You mean like a deer or something?" Wren mused. "Perhaps she can be so pained by loud noises, even voices, that she spontaneously tunes them out?"

"Could be," Kyle agreed.

"That's it, Kyle! That's exactly right. Delphie responds to pleasant sounds, like music. You've seen how she loves to hear Vestie sing and play the dulcimer. But too much noise...and she's gone. Look, Kyle, see how softly Mencie is speaking to her? I've seen Mamaw Zettie deal with her in whispers, as well."

"I wonder what all she hears and knows," Kyle mused, and added wistfully, "Is it any surprise she loves the woods so much? I bet she doesn't miss a thing, and is completely safe there. Nothing could ever sneak up on her."

"No, nothing does," Wren said softly. "Her experience of the woods and mountains is different from ours, Kyle. I know it! I can feel it now, almost as if I can experience the world through her very soul. It's...it's very strange and rather disturbing. It's almost like two separate awarenesses. But I can only tune in on Delphie clearly when her feelings are very strong or vivid, or when she wants me to know something."

Kyle squinted thoughtfully, "Does she know what *you* are thinking or feeling...all or any of the time?"

Wren blushed, "I'm not real sure but it seems like this awareness happens only when there is some kind of mutual consent. It's not a peeping Tom sort of thing. But I believe she knows when I'm thinking of her ...and I know when she's trying to tell me something."

Just then, Delphie turned and fastened her doe-like eyes on Wren. She gave Wren a brief secret smile and then went back to her conversation with Mencie about the herb in her hand.

Kyle rubbed his hand up and down Wren's bare arm as he pondered what she'd just said. "Don't you find this scary, Wren?"

"Well, it's new," Wren began and then stopped and shook her head. "No, no it really isn't. Ever since she was born, I think I was somehow aware of her on some level. I knew her but not in the flesh. Something like being pregnant and knowing you are carrying a little unknown being within you; someone who is part of you but isn't you. Does this make any sense to you, Kyle?"

For a moment, he said nothing. Then Kyle turned to her, "Yeh, it does," he answered sadly with a wistful look in his eye. "It used to be like that with Crowe and me. I always had this sense of what he was thinking and feeling. And knew he was sharing everything I was experiencing, too. It's weird but not so scary. Fact is, it was sometimes right handy."

Wren looked up and grinned, "You don't mean like when you two were taking tests in school, do you?"

"I do!" Kyle blurted out. "We never, ever told anyone how we could ask one another things in our minds during tests, even in different rooms and get answers. He was better in languages; I had the edge when it came to math."

"Wow," Wren breathed softly. "Bet you both did really great in school. You could study math and he could bone up on Spanish and you'd both pass both subjects."

"How'd you know we took Spanish, Wren?" Kyle asked suddenly, grasping her arm more tightly.

"Ouch, Kyle, that's my arm you're bruising," Wren complained. "How'd I know? Didn't you tell me you knew some Spanish when we were talking about how bad things are with the Hispanics?"

"I did but I never told you I'd studied it in high school!"

"How can you be so sure?"

"Because I have never talked about the last few years before Crowe died; not about any of it; not with anyone, not even with you until ... just recently," Kyle said tightly.

Wren felt as if a knife had turned in her own heart. "It hurt you that much, didn't it?"

"It did ... or I feared it would. But now the wonder is that I can talk about Crowe with you and it's just pure relief. I know he'd love you, Wren."

"If he's as much like you as it seems he is, I'm sure I'd love him, too," Wren murmured.

"Just so long as you don't love him in the same way you love me, woman," Kyle joked lightly.

"Just so neither of you tried filling in for one another, like you said you'd sometimes did in class," Wren whipped back.

"He wouldn't dare," Kyle insisted solemnly. "Just let him..."

"Ah, no, I *wouldn't* let him!" Wren retorted. "Dealing with one of you is quite enough, thank you very much!

Kyle pulled his face into a grimace, "And here, I had figured you'd be just overcome with delight to have two of me around; to protect and to cherish ..."

"And to honor and to obey? Well, now, I might could get used to *that*...so long as it's you two doing the honoring, etc..." Wren cocked her head and flung out her arm.

"Kyle, dear, adjust this pillow at my back..., Crowe, my brother, just put that tray right here beside me???" Wren giggled and Kyle tried a sweeping bow which ended abruptly as his heel caught in a rut and he found himself sprawled at Wren's feet.

Suddenly it seemed like everyone ahead of them chose that moment to look back at them. Wren and Kyle blushed red and almost strangled with suppressed laughter as they collected the gear that had tumbled from Kyle's backpack.

They offered no explanation to the rest of the group who kept moving on into the woods.

Wren pulled Kyle to his feet but he did not let go of her hand. Instead he pulled her hard against him and whispered into her auburn curls, "God, Wren, I can't tell you how good that felt to me."

"What? Sitting on your butt at my feet?"

The dancing light in Kyle's eyes faded as he said soberly, "You know what I mean, hon. This is the very first time I've ever talked about Crowe like that since before he died. I feel like he's back with me, with us, I should say, and it's the greatest, the most incredible gift you could ever give me."

Tears glistened in Kyle's eyes and also trickled down Wren's cheeks as she gently touched Kyle's face. "I'm so glad for you, dear, so very glad." Kyle had just pulled back from a deep kiss and Wren was still in his arms when they heard shouting up the path ahead of them. Trees blocked their view so they trotted swiftly up the trail toward the commotion.

They were not greatly surprised to find the cart overturned, one wheel whirling crazily in the air while another went crashing down a small ravine. Hershall and Denver Ray were squared off, shouting and sparring again.

Locke rushed past Vestie, calling out as he flexed his arms angrily, "Don't worry, I'll take care of this."

"Thanks but no thanks," Vestie retorted, as she pushed her way between Locke and her sons. "These here idjits are *my* boys and I'll handle them.

And handle them she did, to everyone's surprise but Wren's. Vestie flew between the two husky teens and grabbed both their tee shirts in her strong brown hands. Whatever she said between gritted teeth apparently impressed her sons so profoundly that without another word, Hershall turned and scrambled rapidly down the rocky ravine to recover the cart wheel while Denver Ray set about collecting the scattered backpacks and suit cases with fierce diligence.

"They'll pay for the damage out of their allowances," Vestie announced to Locke who was checking the axle of the cart and rooting through his pack for some tools. Wren turned her back on everyone simply to hide the huge grin spreading across her face. She felt an immense pride in Vestie for she knew what this cost the normally retiring woman.

Fortunately, the damage was fixable and within an hour, the group reached the parked vehicles on the other side of the notch. Wren and Kyle had followed the Glennings up a state forest road that was off-limits to everyone but forest service personnel and the families whose land had been taken when the Pisgah National Forest was established. Part of the government contract permitted those whose ancestors had settled these coves and hollers to retain access to their home places, especially if these included family burial plots.

Cove folks from Blackburne County who wanted quick access to The Cove could drive deep into the forest and leave their vehicles safely hidden. Anyone who might try to follow them just never located the rutted turn-off for mists would inexplicably spread among the trees and boulders.

Wren watched Locke efficiently store Zettie's stuff under the camper latched onto the back of his truck. He was planning to take his Maw back to the farm in Viney Branch while Vestie returned home over Panther Gap with the boys and Delphie. Wren had joined Kyle in red pick-up when she noticed Locke trying to engage Vestie in conversation. Her heart went out to him. Vestie was listening but shaking her head an emphatic no.

I wonder what that's all about?" Kyle mused.

"I could make an educated guess," Wren offered, "but first, can you tell me what, if anything, Locke may have told you about his feelings for Vestie?"

"He's not much of a talker, Wren, you know that. But from what little he has said, I believe he's been in love with Vestie for years, maybe even before Porter married her. He's mighty serious now about giving her a hand managing the farm...and the boys. But from what we've seen today, it doesn't look like she needs or wants as much help as he's offering her." Kyle glanced sideways at Wren before adding, "She's different today from what she was before you took her back to The Spring.

"Are you surprised, Kyle?"

"No, not all, especially when I remember what happened to *us* when we went back there together."

"We'll just have to wait and see how things play out, I guess," Wren ventured. "Vestie has a lot to process just now and sad to say, Locke just isn't on the front burner. She needs to tend to some more urgent matters before she can begin to consider where or if Locke fits into her life."

Without a pause, Wren deliberately segued into another subject. "Kyle, how do you suppose people are going to react when Mamaw just turns up after being gone for almost ten years? Won't they wonder where she's been? It's one thing for us to be back in The Cove for a few days that somehow just doesn't register on the calendar but *ten years*?

How do you explain that? I sort of figured that once a person...well, retires into The Cove, they stay there until they die."

Kyle tugged on his nose, his eyes following the road but his mind elsewhere, "I get the impression that it isn't done very often... going back to "the world" I mean. That may be one reason why Locke is so upset. I've been trying to work through all that Bewley and Haidia told us and, somehow, it'll be okay. I may be wrong but I suspect that folks are just going to think that Zettie's been living with Locke up at Viney Branch all this time."

"But no one's ever seen her for years, Kyle!" Wren protested.

"No, but no one's going to reflect on that."

"That sounds like messing around with a lot of people's minds!" Wren breathed incredulously.

Kyle sighed, "I don't know how to explain it but people are going to see Zettie and if anyone wonders where she's been, something like the "mist" that protects The Cove is just going to blur their memory of when they last saw her. Don't forget, there's also Cove folk living out and about the area and they understand exactly what the situation is but don't talk about it. Yeh, it's complicated but I guess it works. It's been going on since 1838."

"Whew!" Wren commented profoundly and suddenly put her head down on Kyle's shoulder and drifted off to sleep. She didn't wake up until Kyle drove across the plank bridge leading into their drive and pulled up in front of their deck. Their small home literally hung over the gorge carved out by the Forever River. An ingenious arrangement of supports and buttresses upheld the structure. Seen from across the river, it resembled a crow's nest of an old sailing vessel with the whimsical addition of a red roof and a gable.

Shortly before their marriage, Wren had noticed a For Sale sign on this house which was literally perched on the village limits of Laurel Spring. When she informed Kyle that the realtor had given her the key to view this curious place, Kyle had a sinking premonition that they would soon be signing a mortgage. He was right.

Wren had fallen in love with the precarious charm of this house which, to Kyle's mind, must have been designed by someone under the influence of hallucinogenic drugs. He could only hope the actual builders were not *also* "users." Wren's discovery of some cleverly concealed closets confirmed Kyle's suspicion that the original owners had been

Paul 2019

part of a gang running drugs into Tennessee during the seventies. Drug trafficking was still going on, but this house had been raided too often for it to be a "safe house" for suppliers any more. Hence, the sale.

Kyle and Wren were slowly rehabbing the neglected house and its colorful reputation but most folks still referred to it as the Pot House. A sign board swinging over the bridge was still blank while the couple debated a name for their home. They'd already ruled out Lover's Leap and Suicide Point. Wren cozied up to Wren's Nest – which irked Kyle, while his leaning toward, "Wolves' Den," after his Cherokee name of Gray Wolf, didn't sit right with Wren.

Kyle carried their gear into the house while Wren collected the day's mail. A notice from her ob/gyn for a routine check-up reminded her of something she needed to discuss with her husband. She fried up some catfish for supper, and some okra, which she knew Kyle favored. While setting their table, which was merely a wide plank attached beneath the long windows overlooking the Forever River Gorge, Wren mused on what she really wanted to say.

They had been married for three years and had no children, which until now had seemed fine with both of them. Wed in their mid-thirties, starting a family had not been a priority. But now so much had changed.

Wren was the Keeper of the Spring and although she had left her mother's medallion at the source of the Spring, Mamaw Zettie had given her another one, instructing her to pass it on to her daughter when the time came. Although a thrill had run through Wren at these words, so many other events had happened since then, that Zettie's words were pushed to the back of Wren's mind... except whenever the silver disk brushed her breasts.

Was it time now to tell Kyle about Zettie's words? No *maybe* about it! The sooner the better. But Wren had shrewdly waited until Kyle had finished devouring their supper and his gaze had wandered to the view outside. Before she could initiate a conversation, however, something about her pensive silence alerted Kyle. With familiar apprehension, he asked, "So, what are you thinking on?"

Wren had been pondering several possible ways to bring up their largely unspoken choice not to have children. As she cleared their plates and turned to pile them in the sink, she began, "Mamaw Zettie gave me something before we left The Cove."

"Umm?" Kyle inquired as he studied a group of kayakers maneuvering through a patch of whitewater on the river far below.

"She said I am to pass it on to my daughter," Wren volunteered as she started rinsing the dishes.

"Oh, yeah, 'cause you're Keeper of the Spring," Kyle commented, nodding as the rafters made it through the rocks without dumping anyone into the water. "Each Keeper is meant to pass it on to ...," Kyle choked as Wren's words sank in and the implications were suddenly clear.

"Wren, come over and sit down, will you?" he asked. "I think we need to consider a few things here."

Wren wiped her hands and suppressed a smile. It always worked better when Kyle thought he was initiating a serious discussion. Sitting next to Kyle, Wren reached under her T-shirt and pulled out the medallion. "This is what Mamaw Zettie gave me. I know you understand what it implies but is it something we want?"

Kyle fingered the shiny piece, still warm from Wren's skin. "I guess we've got to talk about that," he admitted. "Are you... I mean, do you really want ..." Kyle stumbled.

Wren took pity on her husband. "I'm not sure that's the whole question, Kyle. The question is: do *we* want a child? You and I? It would mean a lot of changes, many that we had never counted on. I've never given it much thought but now that I am, questions, problems, complications all keep tumbling around in my head. But whether I like it or not, the idea of having a child won't go away."

Kyle settled back in his chair, arms crossed on his chest, knuckles against his lips, like he wished to guard against whatever wrong words might pop out. His silence invited Wren to add. "A baby is one thing. Bringing up a daughter and/or a son is a whole other thing," she mused. "We would be nearly sixty by the time they are grown!"

"And... how would we support them all those years?" Kyle added. "Right now, we're both doing minimum wage jobs... our choice," he added, as he studied the beamed ceiling of the home they were still rehabbing.

"Life was a whole lot simpler before we stumbled into The Cove," Wren sighed. Silence settled between them as they both weighed a decision fraught with consequences neither had ever seriously contemplated.

Kyle finally broke the silence, "Well, I guess if we *tried* for a child but we never got pregnant... that would be one answer to this question."

"Yes," Wren said quietly, "the easier answer. But," she smiled grimly, "what are the odds we'll get off this hook so easily. Nothing about The Cove is ever that simple...."

Suddenly Kyle looked up eagerly, "Yeh, but trying to find the answer could be lots of fun," he announced, and picking Wren up, he swung her off her feet and marched her to their bedroom.

CHAPTER ELEVEN

After Zettie reached Locke's farm at Viney Branch, she looked around his bachelor quarters and shook her head. Locke shuddered inwardly but knew better than to even begin a discussion about his housekeeping. His Maw had always been a force to be reckoned with so he just quietly left what had once been *his* kitchen and headed for the barn, hoping his Maw would quickly, *very* quickly, get so caught up in teaching the women of the Mexican colony that her interest in scrubbing and re-arranging his life wouldn't travel any further than the house. Just to be sure he wouldn't lose anything of value, Locke hastily cleared the back porch of tools and implements he intended to fix someday and secreted them in the barn.

After a few days of quiet thought, accompanied by energetic housework, Zettie announced to Locke, "I think it would be better if I go to the Mexican settlement than if I try to get the women to come into town."

Locke agreed. They had established a colony along the Forever River by squatting in abandoned cabins originally built as temporary housing for drovers and rafters. Most of the migrant workers preferred not to go into Laurel Spring at all for fear of harassment. Unfortunately, Locke knew their anxieties were well founded. If the men avoided the village, it was hardly likely that they would allow their women to venture into it.

"Does Papaw's old farm truck still run?" Zettie asked. "I see you got it settin' in the barn... ."

"Well, I guess I could look at it," Locke offered, trying without much hope, to slow down Zettie's momentum. Whether she knew it or not, she was about to stir up a hornet's nest. The old truck ran fine and he could already see his Maw barreling into Laurel Spring, going from store to diner to Lion's Club collecting whatever items she needed to teach with.

Zettie began ticking things off on her fingers, "I'm thinkin' Spanish texts may be hard to come by so I'll go to the churches and just borry some old hymn books and bibles. I do believe there are some songs in Spanish with English words beneath the text which could be helpful. I'll also need at least one chalk board with chalk and a bunch of coloring books with crayons to keep the little ones busy while their Maw's are studyin' with me..." Zettie pursed her lips, reviewing her mental list, while Locke mentally threw up his hands. He pulled an old bill out of his pocket and began writing things down.

Hopefully, all that Zettie felt she needed could be picked up at the churches and the Dollar Store which had just opened in Laurel Spring. Locke wasn't too certain that all the churches would be happy to donate hymnals or bibles. Certainly Panther United Brethren (PUB) church had no love for the Hispanics but then, Pastor Arlas had yet to come up against a mountain Mamaw like Zettie. Locke grinned. This could get interesting...

To no one's great surprise, Zettie was soon driving around town with boxes of musty hymn books and worn bibles in the back of the pickup. Locke had made a raid on the Dollar Store which eventually donated supplies for the children, as a way to be recognized as an upstanding member of the local community.

Locke said nothing about his suspicion that some movers and shakers in the county would now boycott this new establishment. When he met up with Zettie at the local diner, she was overwhelmed with all he had managed to acquire, which included candy for the kids and fancy hair bands for the women.

Over the diner's justly-famous Mountain Burgers and iced tea, Locke asked if Zettie wished him to accompany her on her first foray out to the rude settlement by the river. Zettie paused before shaking her head. "Thank you but I think, not. I suspicion that a woman will be better received, especially if she looks as old as I do!

"Rather as *wise* as you do, Maw." Locke commented but then couldn't help adding, "All you need in addition to your white hair is an apron and a frying pan!"

"And what do you think is a-settin' in the cab of the truck?"

"Maw, you're joshin' me,"

"No way, son. I'll cook with the ladies as we trade English and Spanish. Can't think of a quicker way to teach them how to get around the supermarket."

Zettie tied a blue tarp over the booty in the truck bed after she left the diner and took off for the Forever River settlement.

Some of the Mexican women began shooing their children inside or behind their cabins when they sighted an unfamiliar pickup heading their way, dust flying after it. Zettie pulled into a nearby field, brakes squealing. For a while, she sat still, observing how the women had set up outdoor kitchens, with flat rocks for baking tortillas and deep hearths where kettles could hang.

Her eyes flickered over the colorful skirts and blouses the women wore and their intricately embroidered scarves. Then she noticed woven fabrics in progress on backstrap looms. Clearly these women had brought their own, rich culture with

Paul 2019

them and Zettie's admiration increased. These intrepid women had as much to teach her as she them!

Zettie had barely eased open the truck's squeaky door when she heard a giggle near her front tire. A further push of the door elicited more sniggers from an unseen audience. She reached behind her seat and tossed out some small bags of candy and suddenly a swarm of youngsters appeared, grabbing for the treats. As she stepped down, Zettie heard "Gratias!" from all sides. Uprooted though these children might be, they were still being taught their manners.

Hovering protectively behind the youngsters stood a cluster of women, some with babies perched on their hips, their dark eyes questioning and unsure. Zettie decided class could start then and there. Pointing to herself, she pronounced her name slowly. "Miz Zet-tie." The children mimicked her efforts, dwelling on the Z-Z-Zies. Picking out a confident looking ten year old, she pointed to his chest questioningly and was rewarded with a grin and a name: Miguel. The girl next to him, she learned, was Gabriella.

Before long, the children were shouting their names at her so fast she could hardly figure out which name belonged to whom. Then Zettie turned to the watching women and lifted her brows. One stepped forward, hands clutched in her apron, and shyly offered: "Marta." A woman cradling a baby smiled and said, "Marianna." When Zettie's eyes traveled to the baby, she added, "Jose." Among the thirteen women who introduced themselves, Zettie met two Marianna's, a Juanna, two Marta's and three Maria's.

With smiling gestures, Zettie was invited into the shade by the cabins where rough tables stood, with a motley collection of chairs, stools, and benches. For today, at least, class would be outdoors where the families probably spent most of their time.

One of the women pulled a gallon jug from the river where it had been cooling and poured water into a pottery cup which she offered to Zettie. She indicated that it had been boiled in the large kettle Zettie had noticed earlier and Zettie's respect for these resourceful ladies grew. They had to care for their families without the benefit of electricity or running water. Colorful laundry was clipped to ropes strung from tree to tree.

Zettie realized that the many plastic tubs and buckets scattered about were prized household items, when two women severely scolded some hapless boys who were turning one into a drum.

"Time to ransack some attics," Zettie thought, remembering toys she had stored away after her boys had outgrown them.

When one of the younger women (was it Maria?) touched her arm questioningly, she responded again. "Zet-tie."

Maria cocked her head and mouthed, "Z-ze-tee?" slowly.

"Si," Zettie responded, using her entire Spanish vocabulary.

She heard a buzzing sound behind her and turned to find a number of small children, running with arms outstretched and miming, "Ze-e-e, zee. Zettie's hearty laugh broke the sudden stillness among the women and soon a babble of voices were throwing questions at her in the mistaken belief she understood their language. "Well, signs and gestures can do for starters," Zettie thought and set about trying to explain her purpose in coming out to the little settlement.

Soon, everyone was laughing as they sat around in the shade, trying to trade basic information about each other. Things grew a bit easier after the older children were dropped off by the school bus. They were picking up English quickly at school and were able to translate some of Zettie's plans. A definite excitement replaced the initial unease.

However, when Zettie learned that few of the ladies had had any formal schooling and were functionally illiterate, she realized her initial teaching method would have to change.

The books would have to wait except those for the youngsters who eagerly accepted the coloring books and crayons.

Once the excitement subsided, Zettie set about giving instructions in conversational English. This posed a new problem for Zettie – should she teach them "proper" English or the more colloquial style and pronunciation of the mountain county? The latter might help them to be more accepted here but how helpful would it be when the families moved on?

Zettie mulled this over as she practiced connecting names and faces. Finally it was clear to her that teaching them "media English" which everyone listened to, would be most beneficial. How long would these women be in Blackburne County after all?

Words of greeting were the first to be exchanged, Zettie stumbling and laughing along with the women as they all learned to form new words correctly, improving accents and usage. "Hello" posed its own problem for the letter H was usually not sounded aloud in Spanish. Learning to breathe it out evoked even more laughter. And Zettie learned to say "Hola" as "Ola". The smaller children were running about slapping raised hands together and shouting, "Hello, Hello, Hola, Hola" with more ease than their mothers.

From some of the older children, Zettie learned that this whole community came from the Mexican state of Oaxaca. The men had been crossing into the US on temporary work visas, laboring in fields and vineyards for many years, following crops northward as fruits and vegetables ripened. Recently they'd begun spending most of the year working tobacco in Blackburne County.

Once the cured leaves were delivered to the auction houses in late November, the men had little over a month to return to their homes and families in Oaxaca. They were expected back to start the seeds from the new allotments in greenhouses or covered with black plastic in fields, by early

February. Some tobacco growers were starting to use a new method which rooted the seeds only in water. Once working over ten months of the year at one site became a steady routine, the men decided to bring their families with them.

The need for hired help in the tobacco fields coincided with the reduction in the size of local farm families. Formerly families had ten or twelve children, who together with their hardworking parents, put in the manual labor that tobacco cultivation required. It was the only cash crop which flourished in the slanted fields of Blackburne County. Also the mountains of Western North Carolina (usually) provided the crucial mix of sun and rain that produced the supple, golden leaf which brought top dollar at the auction houses.

By the time the field workers were returning for the evening, Zettie's students had progressed to "Good-by", "Bye" and "See ya'" while Zettie waved and called out from her truck, "Adios" and "Nos vemos". As Zettie pulled onto the road, she muttered to herself, "Must get a Mexican dictionary or, if possible, one from uh, uh, Oaxaca. I also need to learn to gargle some letters! Time to hit Locke's computer and see what I can find."

CHAPTER TWELVE

Half-way down Honeycut Mountain, Kyle felt his truck start to swerve out of control. He pumped the brakes only to realize too late that he was coasting with a dead engine. Out of gas! Shit! The power brakes weren't responding. Kyle squinted ahead in the hot July sun, perspiration trickling down his temples. There was only one car ahead of him on the long, winding grade dropping toward Laurel Spring but Kyle could feel his truck picking up speed as he approached the bend around which the other vehicle had just disappeared. He mashed down on the emergency brake and wrestled with the steering wheel, just managing to keep his vehicle on the road as he whizzed around the sharp curve.

Kyle recognized the other car all too well. It was driven by Miss Althea, the seventy-some year old librarian who was notorious for posting a steady twenty-five miles per hour at all times. Kyle's speedometer was climbing past forty as his truck swiftly gained on the vintage green Dodge. Another vehicle, coming up the mountain, cut off the option of passing it on the two-lane highway.

Despite the risk of rolling his truck, Kyle veered to his right, toward a shallow ditch and the side of the mountain. Bracing himself as his front wheels jounced onto the berm, Kyle instinctively tramped down on his brake pedal. For a brief salvific moment, the brakes grabbed, slowing the truck's impact into the scrubby brush and rock of the mountainside. Kyle felt his seat belt cut into his breast bone and his head snapped back. Everything went black.

"Kyle, man, you okay?" A ragged voice broke through the darkness and Kyle registered that he was, at least, not dead. Carefully he turned to focus on the anxious face at the window. He knew this man but the name escaped him at the moment.

"I dunno'," he admitted. Slowly, shakily, he relaxed his frozen grip on the wheel and shifted his feet. Everything moved more or less okay. The man at the window reached in and switched off the ignition.

"I saw you swerve off the road jest afore you'd have rear-ended Miss Althea," the man observed. "What happened?"

"Stupid!" Kyle muttered wryly. "Just plain stupid. I ran out of gas half-way down and lost everything."

"*Lucky* is what I'd call you," the man Kyle now remembered as Milt, Iverson's oldest son, responded huskily. "If'n you had to plow the mountain, you picked about the one place that ain't just bare-faced rock."

"Yeh?" Kyle said faintly. "It didn't feel like I had much to do with the choosing." He unsnapped his seat belt and took a few deep breaths. That hurt some and he was aware of a dull ache in the back of his neck. But the rest of him felt whole enough. Kyle opened the door and stepped out gingerly, seeking to assess damages to both himself and his truck. Fortunately, his Ford was a full-size pickup with heavy-duty bumpers and grille.

The nose of the truck was buried in thick, stalky shrubs which had found precarious purchase on the rocky embankment. Milt peered under the front end of the truck and announced that the axle still looked okay. One tire was flat though which accounted for the tilt toward the mountain. The hood had popped up but the engine block didn't look cracked. Apparently that final grab by the brakes had lessened Kyle's speed just enough to prevent more serious damage.

Kyle leaned against the cab willing his knees to stop shaking and his head to clear. "Got a spare tire?" Milt asked.

Kyle gestured weakly. "Mounted under the truck. Can we get at it?"

Milt knelt, and after studying the underparts, shook his head. "I doubt we kin reach it," he said mournfully. "Tell you what. I'm on my way to work but I kin take you back down to Billy's in Laurel Spring. He's got a tow truck. He'll pull you out and bring you on into town."

Kyle smiled gratefully as he slid into Milt's jeep. When trouble happened, you could always count on folks around here to stop and lend a hand. On their way down the mountain, they caught up with Miss Althea's green Dodge, serenely chugging along at 25 miles per hour.

"I doubt she even knew you was behind her," Milt observed wryly.

"Well, I sure did!" Kyle exploded, gratitude washing through him that nothing worse had befallen him that afternoon. "Don't know how I could've run out of gas...seems to me I just filled up before I drove out to Porter's. Fact is I could've sworn I had a nearly full tank when I pulled in there."

Silently he reviewed the chaotic scene he'd encountered. Porter's boys, Hershall and Denver Ray, were facing off with their Uncle Locke who was livid with rage. A sullen group of Hispanic workers closed ranks behind Locke, struggling to make sense of the sharp argument between Locke and his nephews. They didn't need English to interpret the angry gestures.

"You was out to the Glenning place in Panther Gap?" Milt asked.

"Yeh," Kyle pulled on his nose absently. "Suppose you heard that Wren is Porter's niece? She's trying to do what she can for Vestie."

Milt nodded without speaking. A minute later he asked, “You jest back from The Cove?”

Now it was Kyle’s turn to consider silently. Was Milt one of The Cove folk? Even if he was, Kyle knew that most didn’t admit the fact freely. He and Wren – when would they be accepted by most members?

“Pa and I were back in The Cove for the big meetin’,” Milt offered. “Saw you and Wren there.’ He paused. “Don’t know exactly what you did but I’d guess we all of us owe you a powerful lot of thanks. Things looked pretty grim right then.”

“We all do what we can,” Kyle observed blandly, forestalling Milt’s curiosity. Until he knew more about the Cove network in and around Laurel Spring, he hesitated to say much to anyone. Part of the “mission” of The Cove depended on the anonymity of its people. And it was loss of that anonymity which the recent racial troubles threatened.

Milt drove over the bridge and railroad tracks that formed the city limits of Laurel Spring. “Hey, there Billy,” he called out to the stout man in coveralls sitting beside an open garage bay. “Looks like you’re working yourself to death there.”

Billy grinned and waved. "Tough day," he acknowledged, "What kin I do fer youn’s?"

Kyle climbed carefully out of the jeep. "My truck's "parked" nose first into the mountain half-way up Honeycut. Think you could tow me in?"

"Depends," Billy drawled. "If you’n was drunk and thought to climb that mountain in your truck, might jest be better to leave it be fer a bit."

Kyle brushed his hand across his face to hide a grin. The last person to try that was their esteemed sheriff. His truck was still up on blocks inside Billy’s garage.

"Billy," Kyle shot back, "do I look drunk to you? I was out with the Mexican hands working the Glenning’s ‘bacca fields. I might smell like a dead possum but I don't think there's any alcohol in the mix."

The mechanic was already reaching for a key ring from the peg board inside the garage door. "Come along. The wrecker's out back." They were just pulling around the garage when Wren's Civic squealed to a stop in front of the gas pumps. Wren leapt out and trotted briskly toward the men in the tow truck.

"Kyle, that you?" she cried, relief and anxiety mingling in her voice. "I saw your truck wrecked up on Honeycut. Are you hurt?" Her worried eyes traveled over Kyle swiftly.

"Uh, oh, here it comes," Billy muttered out of the side of his mouth.

"Give me a minute, Billy," Kyle grimaced as he stepped stiffly down out of the cab. "Wren, honey, I'm okay, just dumb. I ran out of gas coming down Honeycut and found it convenient to pull off to the side. Got a flat in the process. Billy here is taking me out to raise the truck and bring it in so we can go over it. I don't think there's much damage done."

"I don't care about your damn truck," Wren exploded. "It's *you* I'm worried about. Have you been over to the Clinic?"

"I'm alright, Wren," Kyle began but Wren was running her hands over his neck and asking him to raise his arms slowly. When he winced, she shook her head vehemently. "Kyle Makepeace, you are coming with me this minute. Billy can pull the truck in just fine without you. You and I are going over to the Clinic to see Dr. Blaine. She's usually in most afternoons."

"Wren, I'm just..." Kyle began again but Billy, knowing the ultimate result of this discussion, walked over to him with his hand out.

"Jest give me your keys, Kyle. I'll bring 'er in and go over it. You kin pick it up when you're done at the Clinic."

Kyle sighed and pulled a set of keys from his back pocket. Wren was driving Kyle to the clinic before Billy made it back into the cab of his wrecker.

Later that evening, as lights were starting to wink on in the gorge below their house, Wren and Kyle carried their coffee cups out to their deck. Freshly showered and definitely mellow from the muscle relaxant Wren had insisted he take with supper, Kyle eased himself carefully onto their glider. Never had their home felt so good, he reflected, as Wren curled up beside him, leaning her head back with a sigh.

"A long day, honey," she murmured, her voice blending into the buzz of hummingbirds darting around the feeder hanging over the deck. Kyle agreed, content simply to listen to the gentle rushing of the Forever River as it flowed along its rocky bed below them.

Kyle was slipping into a pleasantly doped reverie when he felt Wren caress his hand and ask, "Kyle, why were you out at the Glenning's today?"

"Locke had asked me to come out – something about one of the Mexican men upset because he'd asked Fr. Bill Daws to baptize his kid and Father had insisted that the parents must come for three months' instruction beforehand.

"Doesn't he know that coming into town after dusk would put the parents at risk?

Kyle looked grim. "I think he does know that and hopes the parents will give up the idea. From what I've seen of him in the past, he doesn't consider ministry to the Mexicans as part of his pastoral mandate in this area."

Wren flared, "In plain words, he's afraid! He doesn't want to alienate his regular parishioners, few as they are, by welcoming the Mexicans to Prince of Peace. I bet he figures there'd be the equivalent of a cross burning in the church parking lot if he encouraged the migrant families to come to Sunday Mass." Wren paused and then asked, "I don't suppose he'd consider going out to their settlement?"

Kyle rubbed his nose, "No, I don't think he will. Neither does Locke. That's why Locke turned to me, wanted to know if I would baptize the child."

"Well, anyone can do that, Kyle. It doesn't have to be a priest. Even I could...or Zettie. Yet," Wren paused thoughtfully, "given the culture the Mexican families come from, having a priest preside would mean so much more. The church is probably the one institution in this country they feel they can trust. What did you tell the father of that kid, Kyle?"

"I explained my position as clearly as I could. He knows we are married and that I can't function publically as a church minister. As far as I can tell, that didn't bother him one bit. All he and Maria want is for their child to receive the sacraments. When I said I would meet them and talk about it, the smile on his face was like the breaking of the sun over the mountainside."

Kyle looked down at his hands and seemed to see the oils that had anointed them gleaming on his palms. Here was another turning in his life's path, a change of direction which, if followed, would restore another piece to his fragmented being. It would also put him in the line of fire – literally. Somehow, that felt like a sort of fitting reparation for his past; a means to amend for his rejection of God and his refusal to serve anyone but his own rebellious heart.

Wren squeezed Kyle's arm, "Am I right? Getting involved with the migrant workers could be dangerous?"

Kyle would have nodded but his neck was too stiff by now. "Yeh, you're right, hon, it could get a little lively."

He fell silent, pondering the day's events. Suddenly Kyle drew in his breath sharply. "It can't be," he muttered but the more he considered it, the more probable it became. Hershall and Denver Ray had been working in the field with Diego and the other men when Locke had introduced Kyle to the small, dark worker. The boys could have easily overheard the conversation and at least surmised the nature of it since it was conducted in broken English, a few fragments of barely remembered Spanish and many gestures.

Kyle had a vague recollection that the boys walked away from the cluster of field hands when they felt they wouldn't be noticed. Could *they* have??? The wheelies they'd been performing on their four-wheelers when he pulled out of the barnyard had distracted Kyle so he hadn't automatically checked his gas gauge.

He last saw them roaring over a rugged track through their upper pasture. Could they have siphoned most of the gas out of his truck to use in their vehicles? If they had, would they have been aware of the danger to which they exposed him? Was it deliberate intent to injure and/or scare him off or mere teen-age thoughtlessness? Kyle was startled when Wren broke in as if she were reading his mind.

"Kyle, how could you have failed to notice that your gas was so low? That's not like you."

Kyle massaged his neck. He stared out across the valley, continuing to replay the day. "My tank was full when I got to the Glenning's because I filled up at the station near Panther Gap before driving over the ridge. When I got there the men were out hoeing between the 'bacca plants. Back-breaking work, that!"

"And hot!" Wren exclaimed. "Vestie has told me how she hates it. But I don't doubt she would have been out there doing it herself if Locke hadn't hired some of the migrants. The boys usually don't do more than a couple rows before sneaking off and leaving the rest for her."

Kyle interrupted Wren, "It all fits, Wren. That's exactly what happened!" Quickly Kyle summarized his suspicions and asked if he should tell Vestie his speculations.

"She's got to assert herself, Wren," Kyle insisted and then stopped. Wren had been cultivating a relationship with the shy mountain woman and had told Kyle what she'd gleaned about Vestie's life with Porter - his careless abuse of her; his neglect, as well as his seemingly deliberate intent to undermine whatever self-confidence she had. As far as Kyle could tell, Porter had succeeded all too well. However, recent events indicated some possible changes.

The cell phone lying beside Kyle and Wren on the glider suddenly jingled, startling them both. Wren arched her eyebrows, mouthing, "Want me to pitch it?" Then she sighed and put it to her ear. She listened for a minute before handing the phone to Kyle whispering, "Gaither."

Kyle wasn't surprised. They had seen Gaither as they left the Clinic earlier that evening. The old man had been dragging his sack of trash to a collection bin behind the post office, the brim of his worn black hat almost concealing his face. Kyle had noticed that the old man was limping and asked Wren to pull over beside him. Before he could say a word, Gaither was asking Kyle about his accident. Apparently the news had hit the gossip circuit while Kyle and Wren were still at the Clinic.

When Kyle explained that he'd run out of gas, Gaither had squinted hard at him. "You ever do thet afore?"

"Not that I can remember," Kyle admitted ruefully. "The truth is I'd filled up just before I went out to the Glenning's. Stopped at the station near Panther United Brethren Church."

Gaither pulled slowly on his pipe, and as he did so, Kyle noticed a large bruise on his chin. Before he could comment on it, Gaither said, "Son, hit's time ah tole you a few thangs." He glanced around and added, "Not here. Ah'll holler atcha later this evenin'."

Now Kyle covered the phone and asked Wren if he could invite Gaither over. Wren nodded vigorously, indicating she had some pie and ice cream on hand. This offer seemed to resolve any hesitancy on ol' Gaither's part and it wasn't long before they heard his uneven steps on the little bridge leading to their deck.

As soon as the three were seated at a little round table with coffee and the promised pie, Kyle prompted Gaither with a hearty, "What's on your mind, old man?"

Gaither had slipped his pipe into his pocket and for a moment, he looked about as if he missed its familiar support when he had hard things to say. Finally he cleared his throat.

"Ah tol' you thet they's trouble afoot regardin' them migrant families. Did you hear 'bout the meetin' over to Creed's place te other week?"

"I did," Kyle responded, "Doc Tanner told me about it."

"Tell ya who all was there?"

"Most of the men hereabouts," Kyle admitted adding, "and Wren learned that the Glenning boys were eavesdropping."

"Pack of trouble, them boys," Gaither grumbled, "jest like their Pa. Don't know but hit's too late to change 'em. Howsomever, thet don't need to bother us jest yit. Ah heerd that Zettie's taken to teachin' English to some of the wimmen and young'uns over at the old Forever River raftin' place."

"Cenia and I help out when we can," Wren put in.

"Mmm, yeh, Cenia's Iverson's woman. A good'n, if ah'm any jedge. Hate to see anythin' happen to her...or you," Gaither added, turning his sharp grey eyes on Wren.

Kyle covered Wren's hand protectively and frowned, as once again, he felt that ominous moment of dead silence within himself that, too often in the past, presaged a catastrophe. "What are you trying to tell me, Gaither?" he said softly.

"Pastors Arlas and Kanardy have bin makin' up a list of folk they call trouble-makers. Ive and his family are on it. So are a bunch of our'n...anyone who's spoke agin goin' after the Mexicans and or bin "conniven" with'em. Even got Doc Tanner down tho, strictly speakin' he ain't one of us. Oughter be, though," Gaither added slowly. "They're plannin' to do somethin' to drive out the Mexicans livin' in the campsite under the bridge and also thosen's out at the raftin' place."

"Who owns those old cabins?" Kyle asked, as he struggled to fit pieces together.

"Wail, it's one of Trevia's kin," Gaither said slowly.

"Trevia's married to Worth, isn't she?" Wren asked.

"She is," Gaither confirmed, "but she and her blood kin are one of us'ns despite that Worth-less husband of her'n." Gaither chuckled for a minute at his own pun.

"Kyle leaned forward, "Who else is on that list? Are we on it?"

Gaither scratched his bristly chin, "Not yet, you ain't. Which means you got to work fast – while it's still daylight, as you might say."

Kyle's eyes narrowed, hearing the biblical imperative in Ol' Gaither's words.

"What would you be thinking I should do?" he asked.

"Wail," Gaither began, once more unconsciously reaching for his pipe. Wren took pity on his courtesy and said it was alright with her if he smoked on the deck. The old man had gobbled down two pieces of her pie which, at his request, were almost buried in ice cream. Wren made a mental note to do this more often.

Once he had his pipe pulling to his satisfaction, Gaither began outlining a plan to bring a number of the migrant workers and their families to a picnic with as many of the local people as they could convince to come. "If'n we eat together and the young'uns play together, it'll be a lot harder to mount a posse agin' em."

"True enough," Kyle admitted, "but where could we hold such a gathering? It has to be a place where the Mexican's will feel it's safe to bring their families and also, some place where folks hereabouts would be willing to go."

"Wail, there's the Panther Ridge Festival comin' up where all the singers and pickers and cloggers from miles around gather," Gaither began. "Sheriff Foch usually runs it down by the hot mud baths near the River – give's the young' uns a chancet to git as muddy as they want and the older folks like the trees and grass and all."

Kyle pulled hard on his nose. "I can't see the sheriff asking any Mexicans to a doin's that he's running."

"Nope, you're right smart there," Gaither admitted with a wry grin. "So we was figurin' mebbe we could git Doc Tanner to have it over to his place this year."

"Will he do that?" Kyle asked doubtfully.

"Thet's where you'ns come in," Gaither retorted. "You'ns know him pretty good and his Maudie jest got Wren here lined up fer a job with Home Health. We figger he might listen to you'ns. Time he stopped tryin' to stand on both sides of the creek at oncet."

Kyle glanced over at Wren who was struggling to overcome her surprise that Gaither knew about her new job for which she'd only done the paper work that afternoon.

"Seems like you're up on the latest, old man," Kyle commented before inquiring casually, "I notice some bruises and are you limping a bit more? What's that all about?"

Gaither pressed his lips tighter around the stem of his pipe. "Had a set-to with one of them Gander boys."

"Woot's son?" Wren asked. She'd instinctively disliked the weasely-looking man and had not found either Brandon or Jason any more appealing than their father. It was no surprise to her that Rilla Gander had divorced Woots some years earlier.

Kyle leaned forward, "Which one?"

"Wail, Jason was settin' out in front of the pub and I suspicioned that Brandon was inside buyin' some hard stuff. Not my concern but when he came out, he was already high on somethin'. Decided he didn't like me pickin' up some beer cans and he jest grabbed my tote, dumpin' everthin' out on the sidewalk. While I pulled at my side of the bag, the other boy throwed his leg out and tripped me flat on my face." Gaither rubbed his chin gently. "Think ah loosened up another tooth."

Kyle felt his blood pressure rising and clenched his fist. Gaither only had about five teeth left as it was. Why did these punks have to humiliate an old man like this? Even as he clenched his fist, Kyle felt a war within himself. Mashing their heads together wasn't going to teach those boys what they needed.

An old adage came back to him with new force: Idleness is the devil's workshop. Someday, if he had the chance, he was going to get those boys into one of his training classes and *then* they would work! For starters, they'd spend a few weeks picking up trash around town – "community service" in spades if he had anything to say about it.

CHAPTER THIRTEEN

The effort to change the site of the year's Panther Gap Festival from the hot springs by the river which Sheriff Foch owned to Doc Tanner's farm was definitely aided by a late spring flood which left the ground around the hot springs slippery and scoured bare – not appealing for most families. Perhaps the children regretted not having a chance to roll around in mud but most of the adults had other visions for a pleasant day in June. A certain amount of leaning on extended family by some Cove members plus some calling in of favors by others soon developed into a community-wide agreement that this year was the time to enjoy the natural beauty of Doc Tanner's place.

Doc Tanner's wife was the farmer in the family and this year she had quite a herd of small horses, as well as young calves, goats, and, oh my, a flock of new-born lambs. A demonstration of how their daughter, Stella, used hand signals to direct their Border Collies to herd the flocks would definitely be an added attraction.

Several deep ponds offered the men trout fishing, as well as a place for the kids to splash around in rubber tubes and rafts. The ladies were looking forward to viewing Maudie Tanner's extensive flower beds where she grew the flowers she sold to local florists.

The main advantage to changing the locale from the riverside venue was the possibility of enticing some of the Mexican families to join the locals in this annual celebration of community, food and music. However, there were contingents on both sides that viewed this "advantage" with deep distrust. Many in the Hispanic community were uncomfortable, not only in the vicinity of Laurel Spring where they'd been shunned but with the Anglos, in general. Doc Tanner's place was a couple miles from the village, on the other side of a mountain but even so, mingling with the mountain folk did not automatically appeal to the Mexicans.

Many local folks usually set up booths to display their quilts, hand carved products, pottery and other wares which they'd produced during the past year. Zettie was encouraging the ladies of the Forever River community to show off some of their colorfully embroidered blouses and hand-woven shawls as well. Despite a gradual enthusiasm for this year's festival, Kyle had also heard some dark grumbles among the men about allowing the "spics" to mingle with their families.

Wren, on one of her routine home health visits to check on Cenia's ninety-six year old mother, was told some disturbing rumors that Iverson had picked up. Some of the men from Panther Gap were angry enough to consider boycotting the festival while others had threatened unspecified violence if the Mexicans dared to turn up.

In an area where firearms were routinely carried, the possibility of serious violence could not be discounted. Even if a majority of the menfolk vowed to protect these newcomers to the county, would any of the Mexican workers risk harm to their wives and children?

When Wren reported these rumors to Kyle, they began to question the advisability of the plan. However, once Zettie learned about their misgivings, she shrugged them off. In her mind, it was now or never, if the county was to become a more united and tolerant community.

"Why am ah workin' so hard with the ladies if, in the end, they's holdin' to their own and never become part of the life here abouts?" she demanded. Via channels unknown to Kyle and Wren, she passed "the word" and soon, enthusiasm for the festival at Doc Tanner's was being voiced on all sides. Although some angry letters turned up in the Blackburne Bugle, the majority of written statements were positive. Fr. Bill, the only Catholic pastor, was leaned upon to write a welcoming piece in the weekly Parson's Column.

Gradually, plans emerged among the women to sponsor a shared meal of local mountain fare and favorite dishes from Oaxaca State. The children, who already knew each other from school, exchanged ideas for games and competitions. A plan for target shooting among the men was quietly nixed, replaced by horseshoes. By mid-June, angry comments lingered only among the teens who felt they might be losing something by letting these strangers in.

Kyle could sympathize, considering the anger he had carried for years regarding the loss of his Cherokee patrimony to the Whites. But he also knew that life never stood still and changes were inevitable. He had noticed that even in The Cove, things were evolving. When he and Wren visited there with Zettie a week before the festival, some new structures were being erected.

Although the traditions of the past would continue to be transmitted to coming generations, the values enshrined in them were already finding new expressions. In fact, next to Zettie's home, a new building was going up, its purpose still a mystery.

The trip back to the Cove had been Zettie's idea and since Locke was involved in running two farms, Wren had volunteered to take her. Kyle had a break in the classes he was teaching and offered to go along. He wanted to talk with the Garonflo brothers about the troubles he foresaw with Hershall and Denver Ray.

Once he had resettled Zettie in her comfortable cabin, she had waved him off to "go study on the new shack" while she pulled Wren down into one of the rockers on her porch.

"Now dear girl, we got us some serious talkin' to attend to," she began and Wren's heart began to beat harder. Did her Mamaw already know what she was only beginning to suspect? Spontaneously, she lay her hand across her belly and then blushed shyly.

"Mamaw, do you think it might be true? I've been so afraid I couldn't ..."

A work worn hand covered hers protectively. "Ah've known since we started back fer the Cove, honey. Yore breedin' a'ready."

Wren looked up into the wise old eyes in wonder and fear. "How do you know, Mamaw? I can only hope this early."

"There be signs, honey, there be signs. A'ready your skin looks creamy and they's a shine in your eyes..."

"Who else but you would note that?"

"Anyone who loves you, dearie," came the gentle reply. "And they's more to this story than you suspect."

Having grown accustomed to surprises, not all of them pleasant, Wren stiffened with fear, not for herself, but already for a being not yet visible to the naked eye.

"Is it?" Wren stopped, "Is it bad, Mamaw?"

"Naw, not this time, honey," Zettie murmured. "But it will ask a lot of you and Kyle."

Wren waited, absorbing the reassurance she implicitly trusted. She needed a daughter to pass on her role as Keeper of the Spring yet Kyle, she knew, longed for a son he could train into his function as Shaman. Whatever the outcome of this almost-too-late pregnancy, she knew they would both cherish their child.

As if reading her mind (as she probably was), Zettie squeezed Wren's hand, "Not child... children," she whispered.

"Oh, no!" Wren's hands flew to her face. "It can't be... you don't mean...?"

"Yeh'm, they be twins," Zettie smiled, with a far-away look. "They's just beautiful," she murmured, brushing a tear from her eye.

"Oh, Mamaw!"

"They's both a boy and a girl comin' soon," Zettie breathed as Wren looked up at her in wonder. Despite the evident delight that Zettie took in imparting this news, Wren caught a fleeting shadow of regret in the old eyes, as if her Mamaw, like Moses, looked into a Promised Land that it would not be hers to enter.

Wren settled back in her rocker, feeling a profound contentment envelop her. Despite the fluttering of her heart, a peace she had never known enveloped her. So much of the future now seemed to rest in her and Kyle's hands but instead of feeling fearful, Wren welcomed the responsibility, a chance to give back and continue what The Cove stood for. Others had dedicated their lives and now...

"Four more lives pledged to the Mystery," Wren shivered.

"Hesh, now, child. Be at rest," Zettie whispered, patting Wren tenderly.

Fragrance from the nearby crepe myrtle wafted over the two women, even as their eyes caught the bright flutter of goldfinches hovering over a nest among the blossoms.

Dreamily, Wren wondered what it would be like to have a home built among the lavender blooms. Without intending to, she surrendered to the weariness claiming her and didn't notice Zettie's hands resting lightly on her head as she slept.

Kyle had found the Garanflo Brothers who were doing the finishing work inside the "shack" as Zettie had called it. Surprised to see the fine carpentry the brothers were producing, Kyle exclaimed, "Whooee, boys, this ain't no shack! Your work looks fine enough for a church."

"As it should," Hall answered, looking up from a clamped board he was carefully mitering.

"Yeh?"

"This here's a'gona' be a place for lotsa' workin'. Ain't all work as holy as prayin'?" Freeman added.

Kyle rubbed his jaw and nodded thoughtfully. "You're right on that, fella's. Do you mind giving me some idea of what this place will be used for?"

"Spinnin'," Hall muttered around a mouthful of nails as he knelt to fit a base board neatly into place.

Catching Kyle's puzzled frown, Freeman pointed toward a partially assembled spoked wheel. "Ever hear tell of a spinning jenny?"

"A spinning jenny?" Kyle asked, "Who in God's holy name is that?"

"What, not who, man! You've likely seen a spinning wheel?" Freeman asked.

"In a museum!"

"Wel'm, there you are," Freeman responded, "That's so old-fashioned we got to come up with somethin' better... only hit's already bin done, so we're just copying one. Here, lemme show ya somethin'." He waved Kyle over to their work bench where he picked up some rumpled sheets of paper covered with sketches and measurements.

"Now, looky. This here's a jenny. See how the wheel attaches to the side of the frame? See how all those threads are running up through here to them eight... whatcha call'em, Hall?"

"Spindles," his brother grunted as he got off his knees and kicked the baseboard with satisfaction.

"Yeh, them," Freeman echoed.

Fascinated, Kyle took the proffered pages to study them more closely. "Where'd you get these designs?"

Paul 2019

"They's taken from an old illustrated encyclopedia of industry which not only give us the piture and idear but even tol' us how it all works."

Awed despite himself, Kyle ran his finger over the finely detailed drawings that Freeman had worked up. "How are you going to power this thing?"

"See here how this pedal pushes the wheel while the spinner feeds fibers of fleece or flax through the holes that separate it onto all the spindles? One person can do the work of eight ... fer a bit."

Catching their excitement, Kyle squatted by a partially assembled frame. "Will the spinner have to stand the whole time? No, I see, you're shortening the legs so someone can sit on a stool ... with a padded seat, I hope!"

The guys chuckled.

Sometime later, Kyle rolled back on his heels, his head reeling with ideas. "You can really spin a lot of wool with a machine like this. You sure you got enough sheep and goats back here?"

"We got some but Miz Zettie says she's goin' to git those Mexicans to pasture more flocks on some of Locke's land. After all, hit's their wimmen who'll be usin' the yarn for their weavin' and stuff."

Kyle pulled on his nose as he wondered if Locke was aware of this plan for some of his pastures. He shook his head. Not his problem, at least not yet. They had to get this thing up and running first. "You guys need any hardware I might get you in town?" he asked.

As the men's voices drifted through the unfinished window, Zettie rocked gently on her porch, nodding. Life would go on whether or not she was here to push it along.

CHAPTER FOURTEEN

"Kyle Makepeace!" Wren giggled, as she rolled over in bed, half-exasperated, half-pleased. "You don't have to treat me like a porcelain doll." Kyle plumped a pillow behind her back before settling a breakfast tray over her knees.

"It's not you I'm worried about, hon. It's our kids I'm thinking of."

Wren studied the single cup of steaming tea that graced the tray where a pink rosebud provided color and fragrance. After returning from the Cove with Zettie earlier that month, Wren had produced a bag of dried leaves and begun brewing the special tea that her Mamaw had recommended for controlling morning sickness. So far, it had proven successful and Wren had avoided the "slump before the bump" that often afflicted pregnant women in the early weeks.

To Kyle's sharp eye, Wren appeared to be blooming and when her ob-gyn visit had confirmed Zettie's intuition, Wren had told him that Zettie had also predicted twins. It was too soon for a medical confirmation of a multiple birth but the couple harbored no doubt that Wren's Mamaw would be proven right. So far, they had hugged the joy to themselves but Wren had begun to feel a strong desire to share their news, especially with Vestie, with whom she felt a special bond. She hoped to see her at the Panther Gap Festival later that day.

Once Kyle was assured that Wren was up and about, he drove across Honeycut Mountain to join other men in helping to set up the grounds at the Tanner farm. Flags were flying everywhere since it was less than a week to Independence Day. This yearly festival usually ushered in a full week of celebrations throughout Blackburne County, with various organizations sponsoring dances, barbeques and the annual baseball tournament between the volunteer fire department and the Grange, with both men and women participating. There was even a Bingo event, despite some grumbling from the Baptist congregation.

As Kyle pulled his truck in behind the Tanner barn, he saw folks pulling out planks and boards from their vehicles, as well as from the Tanner storage shed. Long tables were being set up in a shady orchard; some for serving, others for settin' and eatin', with comfortable rockers for the elders and black tire swings for the little ones. Women were driving in with roasters, Dutch ovens, and bean pots emitting mouth-watering fragrances while some of the men were hovering over a deep pit where hickory logs were reduced to glowing coals.

A carcass of beef hung over the coals and children were taking turns slowly rotating it on a spit. One of the men dipped a brush into a deep pan and spread the sauce, a secret mixture of salt and spices, over the slowly browning meat. Kyle's stomach growled in anticipation and one of the boys grinned at him. "Kinda hard to wait 'til hits done, ain't it!"

"Man, you got that right!" Kyle responded and looked about to see where he could be most useful. Just then he spied a couple pickups parked at a slight distance from the other vehicles. Drivers had stepped out but appeared hesitant to join the melee closer to the orchard. Kyle waved and recognized Migel with two of his boys so he strode over to see if there was a problem.

"We found this board hanging across the road when we drove through the Gap and wondered if folks had changed their minds," Migel muttered. "We were about to turn back but *mi hija* here said we ought to find out for sure."

Kyle turned the board over and could feel his stomach clench. "Spics, go home!" was sloppily painted in red and black inside a white skull.

"We don't want trouble," Migel worried, as he studied the busy crowd. "Specially if we're bringing our women and kids out..."

Kyle nodded, angry lines tightening around his mouth. "Just give me a minute here to see what this is all about." He jogged back toward the house where he spied Doc Tanner coming down the steps carrying bags of paper plates and plastic cups.

"Doc! Have a minute?"

"Why shore, son. What's that you got?"

Kyle silently handed over the rough board and watched as the old vet's face blanched. "Where'd this come from?"

"Migel and his boys found it blocking their way through Panther Gap. They want to know if there's been a change in plans."

Doc Tanner shook his head. By now, a few other men, as well as his wife, had noticed the Doc's grim face and drifted over toward the porch. Without a word, Doc Tanner flipped the sign to face them and a groan of shock arose. Kyle realized that most of those who gathered around were Cove people.

Maudie Tanner grabbed the board from her husband's grip, threw it on the ground and began stomping on it. "NO! This is NOT what everybody thinks," she hollered, her cheeks red with anger. Under her boots, the board was soon reduced to splinters and Doc was patting her arm, trying to calm the tirade which was attracting more attention than seemed wise.

"Not on MY land, not at MY party," Maudie sputtered. She only subsided enough to inform the rapidly gathering crowd about what had been done. "Norie, Cenia, this is somethin' we got to nip right off the branch… if we only knew which tree it came from," she added, gazing over the gathering. Although the smaller children continued their screaming play, most everyone else had turned toward the group by the porch.

Kyle silently agreed with Maudie but had a gut sense that the perpetrators were not present to hear her dire threats. He had his suspicions but, as yet, wasn't ready to tip his hand.

Clearly Maudie was taking charge of the next steps and was already marshalling her troops. In no time, she dispatched the women to commandeer pick-ups and vans. As Kyle watched, they began forming up, two abreast. With a flag raised high, Maudie jumped onto her ATV and pulled out in front. As she waved them forward, the women raced their motors and roared through the Tanner Farm gate.

Soon the cavalcade was rolling toward the Forever River encampment, with the clear intention of blocking any oncoming vehicles. Wren, arriving late with a car load of cookies, did a quick U-ie and fell in with the group. Kyle had no doubt that the caravan would soon return, escorting every man, woman and child from the Forever River camp to the festival. There would be no doubt of their welcome.

Rubbing his hand across his mouth to hide a grin, Kyle turned back to face Doc Tanner and the other men. Many of the eyes that met his were grim. The ladies might rescue today's planned gathering but the guys knew they had to find out who was behind this manifestation of bigotry. They began by eliminating those who had already arrived at the Tanner home place or who were Cove members.

Many more folks were due to arrive later but the group that seemed mainly absent were from Pastor Arlas' bible-thumping congregation. Many of the high schoolers had arrived by now bringing musical instruments and an impressive array of sound equipment. Stella Tanner was busy dragging heavy-duty electric cords out to the porch so the men moved over to the shade of a black walnut in order to continue their discussion.

Iverson rubbed his balding head before resettling his bill cap in place. His wife, Cenia, had been one of the first women to join up with Maudie for the escort/parade. Breaking into some of the quiet murmurs among the men, he offered his blunt assessment.

"Pastor Arlas has got a gang of young'uns hangin' off his coat tail, is mah guess. Many of'em were coached by Porter." he added, voicing the suspicions of many. Kyle nodded and his mind ran back over some nasty deeds he was willing to lay at the feet of Hershall and Denver Glenning.

Although he'd never told more than a few folks that his near-fatal crash on Unaka Mountain was possibly due to having the gas siphoned out of his pick-up by the boys, there had been a few other incidents involving the kids they ran with which cried "Hate Crimes" in bold letters. This seemed like one more to add to the list. The group was acting with an impunity which argued that someone in authority had their backs.

"Well, men, do we act now or wait until the celebrations are past?" Doc Tanner asked, looking around for some consensus. Kyle cupped his chin but kept quiet as the majority favored waiting until after the Fourth of July week celebrations. Before he could voice his deep reservations about this plan, a cacophony of horns drowned out any further discussion.

The women were returning triumphantly with most of the Mexican families loaded in their trucks and vans. He hurried over to assist Wren with unloading some of the crafts and display racks from the back of her Honda. Locke had also hitched on to the caravan, Zettie and Vestie riding along with him. Kyle noted that his hunting rifle still rested on the rack in his cab.

The rest of the day rolled along pleasantly as the Mexican women displayed their colorful garments and shawls in a large booth the Tanner's had provided. He could see Wren fingering one of the softer handwoven pieces with a distant look in her eyes and made a mental note which one it was. No time like the present to begin buying for their future family.

Unfamiliar but savory smelling dishes joined the local fare on the serving tables as Doc Tanner supervised the taste-testing of the side of beef which had been roasting in the fire pit since the night before. Although Kyle had no need to add to his already considerable appetite, he joined some guys testing out the horse shoe pitch. They hoped to entice some of the teen boys to this traditional show of strength and skill by making it moderately difficult but not so challenging as to discourage beginners.

Glancing around, Kyle failed to spy Hershall or Denver Ray among the boys casually pitching a baseball around. He felt a chill cross his neck as if a cloud had just overshadowed the sun but, no, it still shone in a faultless blue sky. Recognizing this as an intuition not to be ignored, he waved to Iverson to join him as he strolled over to Doc Tanner.

"Anybody seen Porter's boys?" Iverson asked, as if reading Kyle's mind.

"That's what I'm about to find out. Doc should know when they planned to turn up. Who do they usually hang with?"

Iverson rubbed his scraggly beard, "Ah'm not shore but seems mainly kids from up in Panther Gap and... (he glanced around quickly) they's a bunch of'em not here! Strange..."

Kyle nodded and quickened his pace. When Doc Tanner frowned about the absences, Kyle sought out Vestie who was tuning her dulcimer on the porch. "When do you expect your boys to turn up?"

Vestie glanced up in surprise. "Why they left home a couple hours before Locke and Zettie picked me up. Aren't they here? I didn't expect Delphie to come but Hershall was on his phone a lot last evenin' and sounded excited about… something…" Her forehead creased as she remembered how the boys had taken the phone out of the house to talk "in private", as they claimed.

She'd felt it wasn't worth challenging them on the secrecy with so much else going down lately but Kyle's unease communicated itself to her. Without further words, they both went looking for Zettie, who was herself trying to track down one of her Mexican ladies.

Marina had given birth a month before and was doing well, delighted with her lusty new son. When Zettie asked about her, the other women from the camp explained that Marina was still in *cuarentena* and would be resting quietly until she fulfilled her full forty days as a new mother. It was not appropriate for her to attend the festival but they had brought some of the shawls she had woven on her backstrap loom.

"Is anyone else in the camp?" Zettie asked, experiencing the same shadow that hovered over Kyle when he reached her side. Gazing up at her tall grandson-in-law, Zettie felt certain something was wrong, possibly very wrong. Before she could ask, Vestie exclaimed, "I can't find either of my boys."

With sudden decision, Zettie turned, grabbed Locke's keys out of his pocket and dove swiftly through the crowds, only her white hair visible when she reached the parking lot. With a running leap, quite athletic for a woman of her age and stature, Zettie landed on the running board of Locke's vehicle, and started the engine before fully closing the door.

Locke was too startled to act but Wren suddenly grabbed Kyle's arm. "Come on, we've got to go. She'll need help."

Holding hands the two sprinted toward Kyle's truck. Iverson punched Locke and grunted. "They's gonna need help, too," and dashed toward his van, Locke on his heels.

"Where do you think she's going?" Kyle asked Wren as he backed deftly around other vehicles and headed down the

Tanner Farm Road, where dust from Zettie's wheels was still drifting. "To Porter's place?"

Wren ground her palms against her eyelids, trying to strengthen some of the ties she experienced with her Mamaw. "N-no, I don't think it's there. She'd just learned that Marina and her baby were still in quarantine at the camp, possibly the only ones still there. I wonder if she's worried about them…though why?" Wren trailed off.

"I'd just asked her if she knew that Hershall and Denver Ray weren't at the festival," Kyle gritted. "I bet she's on her way to the Forever River camp to check on what could be going down out there."

"This doesn't feel good to me," Wren moaned. Just then, a blare from Iverson's van interrupted them. Kyle slowed enough to allow the van to pull alongside. Through lowered windows, Locke shouted that he and Iverson were also concerned about the Latino camp and knew a shortcut through Porter's woods which would get them there sooner.

"Lead the way," Kyle hollered and pulled back to let them swing ahead. Other vehicles were falling in behind them now. Iverson swerved into the Glenning farm, circled the barn and set off across a meadow Kyle hoped was not a marshland. Peering ahead, he could make out Locke directing Iverson toward a gap in the trees where an old logging trail broke through.

It was immediately apparent to Locke that a number of four-wheel vehicles had torn through there very recently. His apprehension now matched his anger at his feisty little Maw who had set off without a word, by herself…in his truck.

Kyle also made out signs of recent passage by a number of ATV's and regretted he hadn't had time to check the Glenning barn. By now, Wren had scooted forward on the jouncing seat, clinging to the dash, her eyes focused but unseeing. Her silence screamed at Kyle to hurry.

Suddenly Kyle sniffed and instantly recognized that the "shadow" was caused by smoke, smoke rising from a sizable fire. Something up ahead was burning and it wasn't Iverson's brakes. His van plunged ahead without pause through a shallow ford and roared up the muddy slope on the other side, a slope already marked by crisscrossed tire tracks.

Kyle muttered, "Hang on, honey!" and followed Iverson's example but tried to mount the further bank at a slightly different angle to avoid miring down or slamming into a tree. Wrestling with the wheel, he caught a glimpse in his rearview mirror of the vehicle behind him slide sidewise and bog down, effectively halting the following caravan. Already men were jumping out of trucks and vans to push it aside.

The light at the end of the tunnel of trees had a surly glow which made Wren's heart clutch. "She's there, she's there," Wren murmured and grabbed the door handle, ready to leap out when Kyle's arm slammed her back against the seat.

"Hang on, hon, we're almost at the camp. See, Iverson's just pulled up behind the truck your Mamaw was driving."

He pointed to where Locke's pick-up stood, motor still running, and driver's door flung wide. Smoke was swirling up from the row of cabins along the river. Young men were busily torching more of the shanties, which old and dry, quickly caught fire.

"Where's Mamaw? Where's Mamaw?" Wren screamed as she threw herself out of Kyle's truck and raced toward the fires.

Kyle's height enabled him to glimpse a head of white hair on the further side of the cabins before smoke blinded him. He lost sight of Wren who was still running despite the dark smoke suddenly billowing out from a window. Probably a can of propane had exploded in the heat. Straining to hear, Kyle caught a fierce cry of anguish from the far side of the burning shacks.

"Who? What?" Kyle's boots pounded the earth as he slipped between two burning buildings and nearly stumbled over a woman that Wren was rolling on the ground in an attempt to put out the flames smoldering in her skirts.

Kyle set about beating out embers flickering in her long, dark hair. The young woman struggled to get to her feet, crying "Mi nino, Mi nino!" Wren's sudden "No-o-o." caused Kyle to glance up in time to see Zettie's small shape disappearing through a fiery doorway.

He pulled a poncho from a line and dipped it into the river. Holding the dripping wrap before him, Kyle rushed toward the entrance, intending to wrap Zettie in it and pull her to safety. Just as he stepped through the doorway, a bundle hit him in the chest and he heard a baby's cry. Instinctively, he cradled the child close and stumbled backwards, crashing into Wren who was about to follow him inside.

Shoving the howling infant into her arms, he gasped, "Take it! Take it! I'll get your Mamaw." Holding the poncho before him, he blindly stepped into an inferno of heat and tripped over something soft. Dropping to his knees, Kyle realized he had found Zettie, pinned beneath a fallen beam, her white hair a glowing nimbus around her face; her clothing glimmering with hot embers. He threw the wet wrap over her, hoping to smother the flames and dragged her unconscious form out into the shady yard.

Wren dropped to the ground beside him as Kyle gently pulled the poncho from Zettie's smoke-blackened face. Although choking and wheezing desperately, Zettie's eyes were open and mirrored an amazing peace.

Sensing the question she couldn't ask, Wren answered, "Yes, Mamaw, Marina and the baby will be fine." A sweet smile cracked Zettie's lips as her hand groped blindly for Wren. Her wheezing struggles weakened and she pressed one hand against her chest. Wren brushed her wispy hair back from her face and wondered if she should start mouth to mouth resuscitation.

But even as she prepared to, Zettie's grip on Wren's hand relaxed and Wren realized that her Mamaw's wise heart had failed. She lay still, the gentle smile still hovering over her lips. Tears dimmed Wren's eyes as she gripped Zettie's burnt hand. "No, Mamaw, no, don't go now," Wren begged. "Don't leave me when I've just found you; when I will need you more than ever."

Kyle rested his hand on Wren's shoulder, sharing her grief, even as he mulled over how the baby had survived. Only after a hand-carved cradle was pulled, barely singed, from the destroyed cabin, did he guess that it had protected the infant from much of the smoke and heat. But how Zettie knew where to find that cradle was beyond his reckoning.

While Wren and Kyle hovered near Zettie's still form, the caravan that had followed them through the woods, arrived. Men and women quickly set up a bucket brigade from the river to the burning cabins, trying to wet down roofs and the surrounding area so the flames could not spread up the forested hillsides. Some of the guys manhandled torches away from Hershall and Denver Ray, as well as from their buddies. Iverson was profoundly disgusted by their manic laughter, realizing the kids were high on pot and (probably) alcohol. This was like a game to them. But not for long.

Sirens wailed as the Laurel Spring volunteer fire department arrived on the scene, together with other emergency vehicles. Marina and her baby were hastily loaded into an ambulance and rushed to the county hospital. Gradually, quietly, folks gathered around Kyle and Wren, who still crouched by Zettie's side. When Locke reached them, he dropped heavily to the ground, moaning, "Maw," over and over.

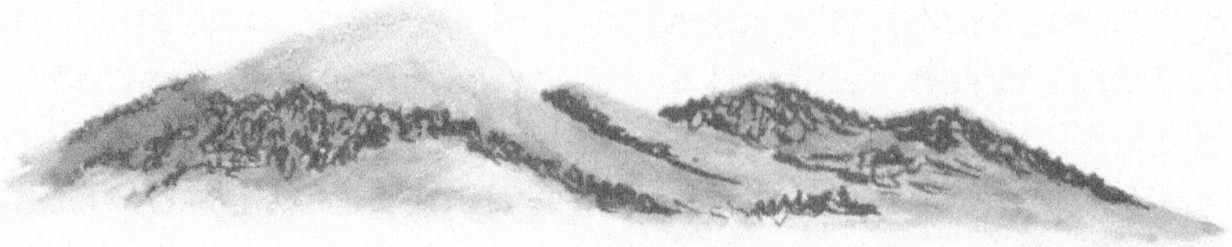

CHAPTER FIFTEEN

"I just never believed she could die," Wren wailed in Kyle's arms, "not, not this soon. I've only known her for such a short time…." Kyle's own tears fell onto his wife's reddish curls as he cradled her against his chest, knowing that nothing could be said or needed to be, at this point. Wren's grief and anguish was only beginning in earnest now, for shock had gripped her in silent composure for the past forty-eight hours.

He rocked her gently as they sat on Zettie's homey porch in the Cove. Pots filled with herbs delicately scented the air with healing essences while bell-like blossoms on the drooping petunias seemed to ring in harmony. If Wren were to find comfort anywhere, it would be here at her Mamaw's where Zettie's presence was so palpable. The past two days had been harrowing.

Once the rest of the festival goers had arrived at the Forever River camp and had dealt with the immediate dangers, shock and dismay took over. A complete assessment of the damage would reveal that all the cabins were destroyed, many to their foundations. Little could be saved from the charred ruins. Marina's husband had set out for the county hospital and soon sent back word through one of the cousins that both she and the baby were in stable condition, despite the smoke they'd inhaled.

Gradually events were pieced together. Zettie must have found a panicked Marina, wakened from her nap in a hammock outdoors, groping blindly in her smoke-filled cabin. Zettie had seized the young woman amid the swiftly kindling flames and dragged her outside, attempting to douse the burning embers on her garments and hair by rolling her on the ground.

Kyle and Wren had arrived just as Zettie was dashing back into the growing inferno. Apparently she had been knocked unconscious by a falling beam just as she tossed the infant to Kyle.

Maudie, an RN, had checked her pulse and would have attempted CPR on the little woman but Doc Tanner shook his head. He knew death when he saw it. While the rest of the men and women helped douse the flames in the row of cabins, Maudie had found a soft rag and dampened it in a water barrel. She gently wrapped Wren's hand around it and directed her to cleanse her Mamaw's smoke-blackened face.

Wren wiped the cloth over the beloved features and was comforted to see that Zettie's expression was not a grimace of pain but rather one of profound serenity. Kyle wondered if this - her last sacrifice - was totally unexpected. Gently he closed her eyes and drew Wren aside as the Mexican men shifted Zettie's body onto the only mattress saved from the fires.

Shoulder-high, they carried her to Locke's truck bed and stood around it as a silent honor guard until Locke was ready to drive back to his farm in Viney Branch. Kyle and Wren followed in their pick-up while many other vehicles fell in line behind them. Although many were Cove members, an even larger number were made up of those whom Miz Zettie had taught over the years.

Some Cove women helped Wren wash her Mamaw's small but sturdy body and dress her in a heavily embroidered huipil, the traditional garment the Oaxacan women wore.

One of Marina's hand-woven shawls, draped around Zettie's head and shoulders, helped to disguise that her silvery white hair had been burnt away. A glow seemed to emanate from her quiet features indicating to the Cove members that her spirit yet hovered close at hand. Kyle, Locke and several other men worked in the barn, fashioning a pine casket from wood laid by for such a purpose.

Word spread through the community that Vestie would host a gathering at her place following the funeral rites set for the next morning. Some of Locke's neighbors brought over a quilt, made in a Star of Bethlehem pattern much favored by the mountain women, to line the finished casket. The service would be held at Locke's place with burial to be in the family cemetery on his farm. When Wren began to protest that Zettie should be laid to rest in The Cove, Kyle silently assured her that it would be so.

The next day proved to be sunny after a rainy night, typical for early July and ideal for tobacco. Despite the usual workload, it seemed as if everyone in the county turned out in their Sunday best to mourn for and honor this little woman whose deeds seemed to attain greater and greater stature as one after another, men and women, stood up to testify how she had touched his or her life. Even the Mexican women, in the halting English that Zettie had begun to teach them, spoke of her and the gentle peace she seemed to carry with her.

As Wren listened, still stunned with grief, she realized that she was being gifted with the memories of two generations to whom her Mamaw had been a living, giving neighbor, mother, teacher or friend. There was much here for her to learn about the woman who was, in every sense, her double Mamaw. As she leaned against Kyle, she allowed the words she heard to slip deep into her spirit, to be brought back later when she could truly savor them.

After the final chords of "Angel Band" died away into the silence of Locke's orchard, Vestie left with some of the other women, to begin laying out the funeral feast at her farm on the other side of the county. When Locke let it be known that only the immediate family would attend the burial, the remaining crowd followed the ladies.

Although Hershall and Denver Ray, as well as Vestie, were immediate family, Sheriff Foch was unwilling to release the boys and their friends from the holding cells where they sweltered in the county jail. Apparently someone had impressed on him that this was not the time to go easy on the "boys".

Vestie clearly felt that it was her responsibility to provide the funeral meal but she offered no protest when nearly every lady turned up with a casserole, a ham, and early vegetables from their gardens, or a dessert to add to what she had been able to cook up throughout the previous night. She knew that she would get her turn to visit Zettie's grave in The Cove at a later time.

Right now, Vestie was pushing her concern over Delphie's whereabouts to the back of her mind, having confided to Locke that the child had not been seen since the fire. Locke had added that worry to the grief besieging him as he washed and polished his pick-up until it gleamed, inside and out. He wanted no grumbles from his Maw about sloppy housekeeping. As a final gesture to her peace-loving spirit, he removed his rifle from the gun rack in the cab.

After the crowd departed, Kyle and Locke had shifted the pine coffin to the gleaming truck bed. Ole Gaither would ride with Locke while Wren and Kyle followed them along yet another secret track back into the Cove.

This trace, running across Locke's land, led through a tract of virgin forest that the Glenning family had guarded since arriving in Viney Branch in the late 1700's. The over story of interlocked giants permitted only stray beams of sunlight to penetrate the gloom near the forest floor.

Navigating with care behind Locke, Kyle failed, at first, to notice an unusual brightness ahead of them.

Alerted by Locke's brake lights, Kyle looked further ahead and felt the hairs on the back of his neck rising. The radiance was not that of sunlight but rather a shimmer of rainbow hues. At times, lavender seemed to predominate; then a grey-blue but its center emanated a strong, steady pink. What the? Braking hard, Kyle saw Locke turn instinctively to his gun rack which raised his apprehensions even further.

When Locke swung down from his truck, hunting knife in hand, Kyle leapt out of his cab to join him. Reaching the hood of Locke's vehicle, Kyle suddenly grabbed his friend's shirt to stop him from advancing any further. A large black bear stood imposingly on the trail, her yellow eyes glaring fiercely. By her side stood Delphie, a small hand resting below the bear's massive shoulder, as if to both reassure and restrain it.

A shudder of recognition shot through Kyle. Shifting Ole Gaither, who had joined the men, behind him, he stepped forward, spread his arms wide and asked quietly, "Belva, why are you here?" With a snort, the she-bear sat back on her haunches and Delphie slipped between her protecting arms. Alarming though the sight was, Kyle intuited deep influences at work here. One more thing was coming together for him. He turned to calm the other men and noticed that Wren had joined them.

"I've met Belva before," she commented mildly. "But why is Delphie with her?"

Kyle rubbed his nose, "Damned if I know! Perhaps Belva's protecting the child?"

The strange glow shifted to blue-grey as Mencie stepped from the shadows. "Thet and more, friends! Don' be fearin' for the gel, now. She's as safe here in these woods as in her Maw's lap."

Kyle shifted his gaze to the other men, uncertain if they were familiar with this fey Warder of the Boundaries, but Gaither was bowing in almost courtly fashion and recognition

Paul 2019

had lit up Locke's eyes. He signaled towards Kyle to take over this confrontation but before Kyle could formulate any words, Wren stepped in front of them.

"Thank you, Belva, for looking after my little sister," she said softly. A sweet smile curved Delphie's lips making it clear to all she was listening intently.

With her usual imperious gestures, Mencie swept off her floppy, grey hat, and explained: "Mah term's comin' to an end soon enough for ah kin feel mah pow'rs weaken'in. Another will take ma place in a bit and hit shall be Delphie!"

Wren pondered this news silently for a moment, studying the three intently. Hesitantly she asked, "Is she not too young?"

"I be young now but when my time comes, I be ready," announced Delphie in a clear, sweet voice no one had ever heard before. She lifted her green eyes to Wren's and nodded firmly.

"Yem," agreed Mencie, "and we'ns be charged with larnin' her all she'll need. Her Maw will be about edjicatin' her in the ways of the outer world; Belva and I will teach her what we know, and all of you will give whatever else is needed." Mencie's piercing gaze traveled meaningfully over them.

Kyle nodded and glanced at Locke who also gravely gave his assent. Gaither stood with his gnarled hand over his heart. Wren leaned forward and kissed her half-sister on her cheek and whispered in her ear. Another smile dimpled her face and a contented rumbling sounded low in Belva's throat.

Before anyone could say more, Mencie plopped her hat on her braids. Belva stood up and shepherded Delphie into the trees behind the wizened gnome, their combined glow suddenly quenched.

Kyle felt Wren slip her hand into his, now wordless after this amazing conversation. Indeed, things were changing. Silently the four returned to their vehicles and resumed their sad journey to The Cove.

As the cortege pulled in through a narrow gap, singing greeted them and continued as a double file of men lifted the coffin from Locke's pickup and in a practiced routine walked forward with men from the front stepping aside as others took their place in the back. The casket was passed to them and carried shoulder-high to the cemetery next to the white church.

"Will the Circle be Unbroken?" carried through the air as all the Cove members gathered, harmonizing on the old mountain hymn. The lid was removed from the casket to allow all the Cove members a chance to view one of their stalwarts for the last time. In a slow dance, everyone walked past, paused in reverence, and placed a flower around Zettie's still form. Finally, Wren came forward and tucked a bunch of late forget-me-nots into her Mamaw's scarred hands. Locke laid a cloth over the beloved face as those around him crooned another mountain favorite: "Angel Band". Then the men gently hammered the lid in place before lowering the casket into the soft earth.

Kyle guided Wren, blinded by her first tears, to her Mamaw's porch where she was finally able to give vent to the grief roiling within her. Her "why's" and "why nows?" gradually subsided with her sobs as she clung to Kyle's warm chest. Exhaustion finally overcame her and she slept, as Kyle laid her down on Zettie's bed.

When Kyle peeked in some hours later, Wren's eyes were open, studying the old beams stretching across the ceiling. "There's such a good feel to this place," Wren murmured, "I always feel somehow protected here." She sighed, "I'll miss this."

Kyle sat beside her and took her hand, "You're talking like you fear you'll never come back here. What makes you think that?"

Wren sat up, pulling her knees to her chest. "Well, won't Mamaw's place go to Locke... a-and Vestie someday? Wouldn't that be only right?"

Pulling on his nose, Kyle slowly shook his head. "No, hon, I don't think so. While you were resting, I talked with some of the elders back here, including Locke, and they all agree that Zettie wanted us to have this place to come back to whenever we need. *Her* place," he added cautiously, "is now ours," and paused to allow what he'd just said to sink in.

Wren's eyes flicked wide, "Oh, no, oh, no, not me, not us!" she sputtered as the full import of what Kyle had said sank in. "I – we – can't take over Mamaw's place. That just wouldn't be right. It's not possible. Besides, we have the twins to bring up..." She lightly touched the barely visible bulge in her belly. But even as she spoke, Wren realized this was why they were given this blessed gift – so they, in turn, could carry on the life and message of the Cove.

Kyle placed his hand over hers protectively, "You got it, honey. Or rather," he added somewhat grimly, "*we* got it. There's no getting out of this story we are part of. It seems we each have roles to play here... all four of us!"

Wren padded into the kitchen after Kyle and suddenly felt famished. She rooted around in the cold cellar, pulling out bacon, the first tomatoes of the season, and a loaf of her Mamaw's bread. "How about BLT's?" she suggested and Kyle set the kettle on a lower flame and went out to harvest some new lettuce he'd spied in Zettie's garden. He was so delighted to see this first interest in food that Wren had shown in days, that had she suggested skunk cabbage and ramps, he would have scoured the woods for them.

He turned to see Wren framed by the kitchen window as she laid strips of bacon into a cast-iron skillet. Unless his eyes were totally deceiving him, he detected a faint shimmer around her and when she turned to pick up a fork, he swore he could also make out two, tiny dots of light glowing in her mid-section. When he almost dropped the pan of lettuce in shock, soft laughter lilted behind and then all around him, composed of voices he recognized from long-past and others he didn't, and couldn't yet know.

A grey shadow flitted across the garden as Kyle re-entered the kitchen – Mencie on her ceaseless rounds as Warder. By her feet, the Dean purred, pausing to sit among the cabbage leaves and clean his paws. Eyes gleaming, he watched the couple in the kitchen. Some things were changing but others perdured. He would watch (and wait) as always.

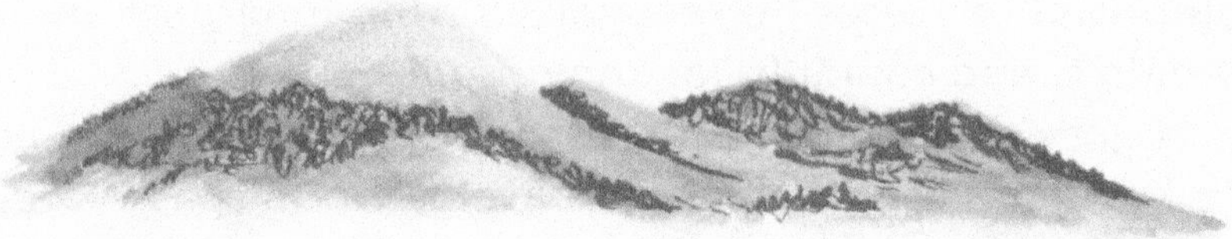

MEANWHILE…

As Wren and Kyle would be told later, the memorial meal for Zettie at Vestie's farm was more festive than grieving and as the evening drew on, singing and dancing began to prevail, even over the eating. Vestie played her dulcimer, joined by various other musicians and singers who not only harmonized on the old hymns but moved on to many well-loved ballads. Among those gathered that day were many of the Mexican families for all of them had been taken into various homes around Blackburne County. Those who didn't have room to house them, donated clothing and beds.

During that afternoon at Vestie's, the men had gathered in groups to discuss building new homes for their Hispanic workers with whom many were developing relationships friendlier than merely that of employer. Responsibility, mingled with some guilt, tinged their intentions.

With some slight urging from Cove members, the planned homes would be scattered throughout the county to avoid the establishment of another ghetto-like settlement. Something new was evolving back in these Smokies, as Zettie had foreseen.

Vestie had been paid a serious visit by Sheriff Foch the day before. Her two boys and their buddies were languishing in the county jail, despite a visit from Pastor Arlas urging their release, for after all, "They didn't know what they were doing." Sheriff Foch had suspected that, whether or not they fully realized the effects of their actions, these "boys" had been urged on by someone who did.

The Pastor's visit confirmed for him just who this person might be. So far as the sheriff was concerned, the young men could linger throughout the hot summer months in the local lock-up (which had no air conditioning) and also, could put in hours of sweaty community service building new homes for those whom they had burned out.

The lawyer that Vestie later engaged on their behalf shook her head, doubtful that they could be tried as juveniles. Hershall was already seventeen; Denver Ray fifteen and most of the other boys about to start their senior year. Arson which resulted in a fatality called for serious prison-time, not just juvenile detention. The lawyer conceded that the boys should each be interviewed separately and tried on a case-by-case basis for she suspected most were followers; only a few were leaders. Her legal firm would handle all the cases, under her supervision.

Vestie's heart was grieved by what her sons had done and sadly – reluctantly - agreed that they had to pay, and pay dearly, for the results of their misguided mischief. The shadow of their father, Porter, still held a strong sway over them. Perhaps, over time, and with the influence of leaders from the Cove, they might be able to see their arson as the racist act it was and not just a defense of their "homeland" and familiar way of life. As Appalachian boys in the state prison system, they might well experience what it was like to be on the receiving end of discrimination.

Unknown to Vestie, one person in the crowd of feasters, was a reporter from the nearby city of Lashton. The story he ran in his paper was picked up by the wire services and spread across the country. He had ended his account with a description of the "old-timey" ballads and dancing which rounded out the celebration of a woman whose life had apparently touched every living soul in the county. Intrigued, a local recording company decided to check out the possibilities of producing a DVD of the balladeers of Blackburne County, featuring Vestie on the dulcimer and as lead singer.

As lanterns were hung along the eaves of the porch, Vestie, her cheeks bright with the joy of her music, looked around for Locke, before remembering that he would be back in the Cove. She missed him, not just as a backup singer but as the kind of person she could trust. Delphie had slipped out of the woods and now stood shyly by her side, relieving one burden from her heart. Perhaps she was the best thing Porter had ever given to the community he both loved and hated. Healing would take time but Vestie felt the power and will for it enfolding her. From somewhere behind her, she could hear Zettie's foot, tapping time to the music.

A subtle glow enveloped the dancers and singers, the glow of a life energy stronger than the forces of violence or hatred. What was cradled here in this holler merged with other centers where life and willingness to love flourished. Darkness could not, would not, overcome it.

Questions to Ponder and Share

Whenever we commit ourselves to personal change and growth, as Kyle and Wren did, we are challenged to help rectify problems outside ourselves. Name some of the Involvements that claimed them. Have you experienced a call to personal growth and discovered that you are asked to give a hand to a neighbor in need?

Various spiritual practices are described throughout the book. What resonated with you? Which ones turned you off?

Which character in the story would you like to befriend? What role do the Elders in the Cove play in addressing the problems in Blackburne County?

Can you see the truth of the Cove and even the possibilities for such enclaves, hidden in plain sight perhaps, to bring about a better life in the future?

Has the Cove drawn you in? Do you feel summoned to follow the spiritual calling of *your* heart; *your* soul?

Let us talk. Let us share. You can reach Paul and Karen, plus other readers at www.ravensbreadministries.com/blog Or via email: pkfredette@frontier.com

Paul and Karen Fredette
18065 NC 209 Hwy.
Hot Springs, NC 28743
PH: 828 622 3750